Topi S[

RAHI MASOOM RAZA

Translated by Meenakshi Shivram

With an Introduction by Harish Trivedi

OXFORD
UNIVERSITY PRESS

OXFORD
UNIVERSITY PRESS

YMCA Library Building, Jai Singh Road, New Delhi 110 001

Oxford University Press is a department of the University of Oxford. It furthers the
University's objective of excellence in research, scholarship, and education
by publishing worldwide in

Oxford New York

Auckland Cape Town Dar es Salaam Hong Kong Karachi Kuala Lumpur
Madrid Melbourne Mexico City Nairobi New Delhi Shanghai Taipei Toronto

With offices in
Argentina Austria Brazil Chile Czech Republic France Greece Guatemala
Hungary Italy Japan Poland Portugal Singapore South Korea Switzerland
Thailand Turkey Ukraine Vietnam

Oxford is a registered trademark of Oxford University Press
in the UK and in certain other countries

Published in India by Oxford University Press, New Delhi

© Oxford University Press 2005

The moral rights of the author have been asserted
Database right Oxford University Press (maker)

ISBN 019 567089 2

MR. Omayal Achi MR. ArunachalamTrust was set up in 1976 to further education and
health care particularly in rural areas. The MR. AR. Educational Society was later
established by the Trust. One of the Society's activities is to sponsor Indian literature.
This translation is entirely funded by the MR. AR. Educational Society as part of its aims.

Typeset in Gary Owen 10/12 by Jojy Philip
Printed in India by Mahalaxmi Printer, New Delhi -110 020
Published by Manzar Khan, Oxford University Press
YMCA Library Building, Jai Singh Road, New Delhi 110 001

Contents

Foreword

Writing this novel has not been a particularly happy experience. For suicide is symptomatic of the failure of a civilization. But Topi had no other alternative. I, too, am like this Topi and there are many others like me. There is just one difference between people like us and Topi. Sometime or the other, for some reason or the other, we end up making compromises. And that is why we continue to live. Topi was not a God nor a Prophet. But he did not make compromises. And so he committed suicide. Exactly as in *Aadha Gaon*, this too is not a story of one person or a group of people. This too is a story about Time. The hero of this story too is Time. It only befits Time and none other to be the hero of any narrative.

Aadha Gaon was filled with abuses. There is not a single swear word in Maulana *Topi Shukla*. Perhaps because this entire novel is an abuse in itself. And I have openly declared this abuse from the very rooftops. This novel is obscene—just like life!

RAHI MASOOM RAZA

Remembering Masoom
A Note by the Late Author's Wife

My friend, Mini Krishnan, who edited this translation has asked me to write about Masoom—but what should I write? I have no idea what to say, for this place I now occupy belongs rightfully to Masoom. Anyway, Rahi Masoom Raza—who has been Masoom to me and family members and Papa to his children—had an extremely different style and method of work. Perhaps I could tell you something about the way he worked.

Masoom could never write anywhere other than at home. He used to say that unless he heard familiar voices and sounds of people at home, and unless he saw the faces of his family members, he could not write. It was here that he could write comfortably. Only here. And this was really a wonder—for the house was always so noisy. One could hear pop music blaring from Aaftaab's room and Ghulam Fareed's *qawwalis* would waft in from the balcony—but all these would not disturb Masoom. He would remain engrossed in his work. Usually, Masoom would be on the carpet— half-sitting, half-lying, a pillow for support, a few files spread open in front of him—and he would be writing. He would work on one file, and after some time, he would close that file and start working on another.

I had once asked him how he could work on different stories at one time. He had replied, 'I have trained my mind in such a way that when I finish doing a part of one work, I switch off that part in my head and begin work on the next thing.' This would be his schedule for hours. During this time, he would also meet people—people who came to meet him, people who had work with him; there would be time for small tasks and time to talk shop as well. Some would come over to discuss a new project and then soon it would be evening.

Masoom never worked during the evening hours for this was the time he kept aside for his family. We always had dinner together. And Masoom always loved to have guests for dinner, so that was how it would often be. Whenever Masoom had to do serious work, like writing a novel, he would do so after midnight. He would work through the night. He would never go to bed before three in the morning. And it was also important for him to be up by seven, so that he could have breakfast with his children—Aaftaab and Mariam—as the children would have to leave for school by eight.

This is how, from 1966 to 1992, Masoom wrote the scripts for over two hundred films, innumerable articles for newspapers and magazines, and novels like *Topi Shukla, Himmat Jaunpuri, Scene 75, Katra Bi Arzu*. Along with these, he also wrote scripts for TV serials. In the midst of all this, he also found time for *shaayari*, and two collections of his poems, *Main Ik Pheriwala* and *Gareeb-e-Shehar*, were published in Bombay.

I am grateful to Masoom's closest friend and brother, Dr Kunwar Pal Singh and his wife, Lalita Bhabi, for being our support at all times. I'm not a writer. I've written this in the uneven and unlettered way I know and is mine.

NAYYAR JEHAN

Translator's Note

I was in the not unusual state of a post-Ph.D. euphoric emptiness when Dr Raza's novel was commissioned to me. I read the first few lines just to make sure that the novel was indeed in Hindi and not in the Urdu that Dr Raza is wont to employ frequently. Having accepted the brief, I learnt my first lesson then that novels, like novelists, are not the most predictable of beings. This novel was in Hindi but it was about Hindi and Urdu, it was about words and how they are pronounced, about linguistic cultures that have forgotten their origins. In the very first page I was confronted with what is truly a translator's second nightmare—a clarification of how a word ought to be pronounced; the first, of course, being a punning on words!

In every chapter there has been a phrase, a metaphor, or the use of a dialect form that has appeared as a translator's stumbling block. For instance, Dr Raza speaks nonchalantly of the *shareef* Hindu, a shareef Muslim, and ends with a pun on Bihar Sharif—how else, if not with a footnote, can this be rendered in translation? Are footnotes then indicative of a failure to translate? Should footnotes be seen as a bridging between languages or as the demons that divide languages? Even if used only as a last resort, do footnotes impede the process of translatability?

Soon, however, the whole process of translating became a game between the writer and the translator, and each time that one found a way to counter the writer's calibrated linguistic calisthenics, the pleasure in the game deepened. One felt not unequal to the writer.

Till one reached the penultimate chapter. . . .

Here Dr Raza twists the phrase—*yeh mooh aur masoor ki daal*—to create a sparkling comedy of words and here the translator lost hands down. There was no way in which the modified phrase could be translated and there was no ready alternative to that phrase in English. This joke sadly defied footnoting as well—how does one explain a funny remark except by saying that it is funny? The only gratifying thought was that the authority of the original remained unarguably settled—the author rightfully won this game.

Dr Raza uses a very simple language and very short sentences. I have tried my best to retain those stylistic elements. There were moments of temptation when one tried to make Dr Raza sound better. Using words like 'explained' instead of the simple 'said', but one fought to resist these attempts at 'improving upon' Dr Raza's definitive linguistic choices.

A note about the use of Indianisms would not be out of place here. 'Indianisms' are often seen as being grammatically awkward, unrefined, and jarring, if not misleading, to an ear trained to carry the burden of 'correctness'. My own preference, however, has been to stick with the very quaint use of Indian phrases. There is a moment in the novel when Topi, unable to clear his exams as he was ill with typhoid, decides that the next year he would clear his exams whether he had typhoid or 'typhoid *ka baap*'. After several drafts and re-writes one succumbed to de-Indianizing this phrase and making it sound 'propah'. However, a few chapters later, there is an argument over who this country belongs to—does it belong to the Hindus at all? Topi's remark to his dissenting friend is: 'Does it belong to your father?' This patriarchal notion of ownership and power is seen in everyday speech and I have thought it best to translate it literally. There are other phrases: '*Lalaji ki aankhen khuli*' (Lalaji's eyes opened)—which is different from '*Lalaji ne aankhen kholi*' (Lalaji opened his eyes). Here, I have chosen to go with the second alternative. The explanation provided here is not meant to silence critics who would see the use of Indianisms as a justification for poor translation. This is being mentioned only in order to state that the translator makes choices, knowingly.

If this note focuses so much on Raza's language, it is only because I think it is important for every translator to be able to make some observation that will contribute towards a fuller theorizing of translation studies. This novel is assuredly more than just about language. It is about intolerant societies, it is about uncompromising individuals whose spirits get broken in the face of such unchanging intolerance, it is about history's inability to teach mankind any useful lessons. This is a story set in the Aligarh of the sixties, but its relevance remains just as immediate and as undiminished in a post-Godhra India. This is a story about people like Topi; it is also, more tragically, about people like Topi's mother, Ramdulari. This story tries to understand the psyche of Uttar Pradesh with its very Muslim Aligarh, its very Hindu Benares, and their exotic confluence in Lucknow. For theory buffs, there is a great deal of intertextuality and metafiction as well!

Readers familiar with this writer's works in the original call him not Dr Raza, but Rahi Saheb. This is perhaps what translation into the English language does—it sometimes tends to make things antiseptic clean. It robs a certain familiarity and replaces it with a respectful distance, but I don't think it ever distorts.

Translating this book has been a challenge—to say the very least. For this, I'd like to thank Mini Krishnan for her faith in me. Unless one has access to the drafts, there is very little evidence of the work done by the editor. Mini has all along been a crusader for translation studies and very often she has fought her battles alone. Poring through each word of the manuscript, she works along with, and as much as, the translator does. Mini's invisible ink pervades this entire translated version.

Thanks are due to two other women who have directed my attention towards translation studies—Dr C.T. Indra and Geeta Dharmarajan. The author's wife, Nayyar Jahan Reza, was always available for her comments and inputs. I'd like to dedicate this English rendering of Dr Rahi Raza Saheb's work to my mother, Mrs. Laxmi Narayanan, my very first and finest story-teller.

MEENAKSHI SHIVRAM

Acknowledgments

For information about Rahi's life and works, I have drawn mainly on a special issue on Rahi, of the journal *Abhinav Kadam* (5: 6–7, November 2001–October 2002, p. 518), re-edited and reprinted as a book under the title *Rahi aur Unka Rachna-Sansar* (Delhi: Shilpayan, 2004). Both publications were edited by Professor Kunwar Pal ('K.P.') Singh, lifelong friend of Rahi. 'I am Topi Shukla!' Professor Singh told me when I met him, later specifying that the character of Topi Shukla was based about 'eighty per cent' on him. When Singh read the novel in manuscript in 1967, he had protested to Rahi against the ending of the novel which has Topi commit suicide, and Rahi in response had said he would have no objection if Singh could propose another ending which would save Topi. (Personal communication, 9 February 2004.)

Introduction

Rahi Masoom Raza (1927–92) occupies a special place in the front rank of the Hindi novelists who began to write after Independence. His first novel, *Adha Gaon* (1966), created a sensation shortly after publication, as it told the unadorned and often unpalatable truth about Muslims and Hindus and the creation of Pakistan in a shockingly earthy and authentic language. In a prompt acknowledgment of its bold originality, the radical Hindi critic, Namvar Singh, then Professor of Hindi at the University of Jodhpur, put it on the M.A. syllabus of that university in 1972, but then found that he was as promptly forced to withdraw it. The novel was charged with being both communalist and obscene.

The controversy, however, laid the foundation of Rahi's lifelong reputation as a fearlessly secular writer, a reputation he steadily consolidated through his second novel, *Topi Shukla* (1968), the six other novels that followed over the years, and a constant series of outspoken public interventions in the cause of combating both Hindu and Muslim communalism. He had worked for a living all this while as a scriptwriter for Hindi films, and his secular commitment and lifetime endeavour received the widest possible public acknowledgment and acclaim when he was asked to write the script for the TV serial, *Mahabharat*, to reinvent an epic which has been a foundational text of the Hindu/Indian civilization for over two millennia. This latest retelling of the epic in a new medium in Rahi's version, which focused not only on action but also on reflection, proved to be phenomenally successful, reaching an audience far larger probably than any other version had reached before.

LIFE

Rahi Masoom Raza, as he came to be known, was born Syed Masoom Raza Abidi on 1 August 1927, in the village Gangauli, in the Ghazipur district of eastern UP. He came from a family of small landowners and was brought up in Ghazipur where his father was a highly successful lawyer in the district courts. Rahi contracted tuberculosis at a young age and spent much of his childhood at home and for long stretches in bed; he was later to say that he hadn't had much of a childhood nor much of a teenage. However, he recovered completely and was sent for higher education to the Aligarh Muslim University, an obvious destination not only for him but also for all his brothers.

He studied Urdu literature at university, obtaining a first division and standing first in his M.A. examination, and then proceeded to write a Ph.D. thesis on 'Glimpses of Indian Life in *Tilism-e-Hoshruba*'; this may be regarded as an early indication of his constant project to look on Islam as located not in some other land far away but right here in India and as belonging here. Meanwhile, he had taken to Aligarh in a big way. He had begun to write poetry under the pen-name 'Rahi' (which means a way-farer) and, unusually, he put his *takhallus* not after his name but before it. (As a member of the Communist Party, he had dropped the title 'Syed' and his surname 'Abidi' as being indicators of the class he came from.) Both as a poet and as a person, he seems to have won an exceptional measure of popularity among his peers, including young women, for whom even his limp (the one remaining marker of his tuberculosis) apparently proved to be a Byronic point of attraction. By the time he began to teach as a temporary lecturer in the Urdu Department at the university, Rahi seems to have become a confirmed and devoted Aligarhian.

This did not last. After having taught initially as a research student and then as a lecturer for six years, Rahi was rejected for a permanent appointment, a decision which he believed till the end of his days to be unforgivably unfair. Meanwhile, he had married Nayyar Jahan, a divor-cee. The consequence of both these developments was that Rahi felt obliged to leave Aligarh, his city of youthful enchantment, a Shangrila of cohesive culture, which he could never stop writing about in his fiction as well as his poetry. One of his best poems is a poignantly evocative ode to this forced separation, titled *Chand to ab bhi nikalta hoga* (Surely the moon still rises on that city).

The remaining three decades of Rahi's life were spent in the world of Hindi films in Mumbai. Following a path only too well–beaten by Urdu writers especially of a progressive persuasion, Rahi struggled to set himself up as a writer for Hindi films, initially unable to decide whether his talent lay as a writer of lyrics or of scripts. Many Urdu writers before him, such as Sahir Ludhianvi, Shakeel Badayuni, Majrooh Sultanpuri, Ali Sardar Jafri, and Kaifi Azmi, had gone to Bombay and written lyrics for Hindi films, which have been traditionally composed in a frozen vocabulary of Urdu eroticism. But Rahi struck out to make a place for himself as a writer of scripts, such as several eminent Hindi novelists, including Premchand, Bhagvati Charan Verma, and Amrit Lal Nagar had tried to do before him but then given up out of disgust with the vulgarity and commercialization of the medium.

Rahi, however, made a go of it, though complaining all along how scriptwriters in the world of Hindi films were regarded as worse than useless. He wrote the script for over two hundred films, successfully enough apparently to have even been raided by the income tax department, and yet felt that his heart lay in creative writing which he continued to nourish on the side against all odds. He consoled himself by saying that he tried to compensate for the lucrative hack-work he did; first, by trying to protect at least a little corner in most films he wrote where he could say something meaningful of his own and, second, by making time in the midst of all his other preoccupations to keep the stream of his novels and poetry flowing, independently of his writing for films. He may have given hostages to fortune, but he did not pay as ransom all the talent he had.

All through his years in Mumbai, Aligarh glimmered as the bittersweet object of his undying desire and nostalgia. If Mumbai represented the demands of the world upon himself, what Ghalib called *gham-e-rozgaar* (the sorrows of the mundane world), Aligarh stood for *gham-e-ishq* (the sorrows of love). In a premonition, in a poem called 'Vasiyat' (Last Will and Testament) that Rahi had published in 1963 before he left Aligarh, he anticipated dying far away from home in a place where no one understood his language or appreciated his manner of narration and where his art had been bitten to death by the she-snakes of coffee-houses and drawing-rooms. He wished that he would, eventually, be buried by the river Ganga in the village (named after the river) where he was born, Gangauli.

This wasn't to be, and Rahi was buried where he had lived for so long, in Mumbai. However, just a few months before he died on 15 March 1992, there had been a home-coming of sorts, when he returned to Aligarh to give a lecture at the university there on 25 November 1991. He began by saying how it was an especially significant day in his life, for the university had, by inviting him, applied balm to an old wound inflicted twenty-five years ago. Of all Rahi's novels, *Topi Shukla* contains probably the fondest fictional evocation of his days in Aligarh and how abruptly they had to come to an end.

WORKS

Rahi's first novel, *Adha Gaon* (translated into English by Gillian Wright initially under the unfortunate title, *The Feuding Families of Village Gangauli*, 1995, and later reprinted as *Half a Village*, 2003), was such a stunning success as to suggest that it might well be the one novel which Rahi had it in him to write. The literary history of the world is full of writers who wrote either only one novel or went on rewriting that first novel for the rest of their careers without knowing it. But though Rahi never again wrote a novel to equal the acclaim won by *Adha Gaon*, he proved with his very second novel, *Topi Shukla*, that he also had another entirely different world to write about and in a very different idiom and style. If his remaining six novels are generally seen as a falling off, it is not because Rahi does not invent new locales, situations, and characters in them, but because whatever the locale and situation, he keeps, for the most part, returning in one way or another to the thematic and emotional ground he has already staked out in his first two novels.

Adha Gaon is set in the village Gangauli, or more accurately in the Muslim half of that village which Rahi knew well; hence the title. It is always the time of Moharram in the village when those who have left the village to go and live in towns return to it year after year to mark in the traditional way the rituals of mourning. It is the mid-1940s and Pakistan is in the offing; young students from Aligarh visit the village to try and convert the bemused villagers to their separatist cause and are met with open scorn. Pakistan comes into being anyway, and some of the characters even migrate to it, but for those who have stayed behind, the abolition of *zamindari* shortly afterwards is shown to be a no less transformative event. In the world of *Adha Gaon*, this affects the living relation between the men and the land rather more than Partition, which happens off-stage in dim, dubious, and distant circumstances.

Topi Shukla, in contrast, is set not in a village but in the city of Aligarh, and not at the cusp of Independence but about fifteen years later, in the early 1960s, when the dust of Partition is supposed to have settled, except of course that it hasn't. While *Adha Gaon* was almost entirely Muslim in its dramatis personae and ambience, *Topi Shukla* has for its eponymous hero a Hindu. Pakistan is already a reluctantly accepted reality, and still casts a long shadow on the Muslims who have stayed behind and look on it alternatively as a utopia or dystopia. While some of them still, at moments, toy with the idea of crossing over to Pakistan, the major issue for them now is rather how to remain and coexist. *Topi Shukla* as a novel is so differently conceived from *Adha Gaon* as not to seem even a distant cousin of it, much less a sibling or sequel.

Similarly, the novels that followed *Topi Shukla* seem quite distinct from Rahi's first two novels as well, at least in outward detail. *Himmat Jaunpuri* (1969), set in Jaunpur, Ghazipur, and Mumbai, is an intimate depiction of the life of Indian Muslims and shows how caste in India transcends religion, so that even when one has converted to a more egalitarian religion such as Islam one still carries the old baggage. *Oas ki Boond* (1970; A Dewdrop), a shorter novel, is about a Hindu temple which is looked after by a Muslim family as its forbearers had built the temple before they converted to Islam; it also has a distinctly secular character saying (in English): 'Secularism! How I hate this word.' *Dil Ek Saada Kaagaz* (1973; The Heart is a Blank Sheet), a more ambitious if also more diffuse narrative, begins with the protagonist's innocent but sexually inquisitive childhood in Ghazipur and then moves on to his half-willing exploitation as a script-writer for films in Mumbai, while bearing witness to the pervasive corruption of politics and the formation of Bangladesh. *Scene 75* (1977), as the title signals, is focused on the Hindi film world in Mumbai and populated largely with directors, scriptwriters, actors, and actresses, each seedier and more cynical than the other.

Katra Bi Arzu (1978), set in Allahabad, has the bulldozer of the Emergency rolling through it over the claims of the poor, while the better-off classes collaborate with the powers that be; it is one of the few novels in Hindi depicting the Emergency, as distinct from the numerous poems. Rahi's last published novel, *Asantosh ke Din* (1986), set in Mumbai and again to do with the forces of communalism and regionalism, engages with the recent manifestation of the Hindu-Sikh riots as a variation on and extension of the Hindu-Muslim riots. When he died, Rahi left unfinished an ambitious novel, *Master Brajmohan ki Karmabhumi* (Master Brajmohan and his Arena of Action), intended to be a saga of three generations spanning the period since 1942. His numerous other works in various genres include *1857: Kranti-katha*, a verse narrative of the Mutiny, and *Chhote Aadmi ki Bari Kahani* (The Great Story of a Little Man), a biography of Abdul Hamid who won the Param Vir Chakra for fighting courageously to death in the 1965 war against Pakistan.

NARRATIVE STYLE: THE NOVEL AS *QISSA*

Throughout these various works, Rahi shows an urgent engagement with the burning issues of the day in a way that is radically committed and palpably purposive. (Indeed, such was the extent of his Marxist allegiance in his fervent youth that in a local election in Ghazipur, Rahi and his elder brother Moonis Raza campaigned resolutely against their own father to ensure the victory of the Communist candidate.) But what distinguishes Rahi's novels from a lot of other propagandist fiction and makes them more acceptable and appealing is Rahi's unique manner of narration, his *andaz-e-bayan* as it is called in Urdu. It derives unmistakably from the oral mode of *qissa-goi*, a tradition of telling tales in which the charm of the tale lies in its telling, and the teller constitutes as great a source of enjoyment for the audience as does the tale itself. The story often begins one way and then proceeds another, new characters and seemingly unrelated episodes proliferate right through, digressions are the rule rather than the exception, and therefore mustn't even be thought of as digressions. The narrator has every right to hold up the tale whenever he likes in order to deliver thoughts and opinions of his own; the spontaneous and often humorous narratorial tone sustains a direct, warm, and informal address to the listener; and finally, a clearly deduced moral hangs by every tale which makes it more than mere entertainment.

Though Rahi, of course, did not orally narrate his novels like the old qissa-gos (or as Hindi film script-writers and directors apparently still do to their actors and producers), he clearly retained some of the old flavour and manner and also some of the advantages which the modern Western novel, with its notions of an organic plot, material and psychological realism, and consistent characterization, does not possess. In any sustained discussion and theorization of how the Indian novel has remained distinct from the Western novel, not because of a failure to imitate it perfectly but because, with its different genius, it has chosen not to follow that model blindly, the novels of Rahi Masoom Raza will prove to be valuable evidence. His appreciation of the older, magical series of tales, *Tilism-e-Hoshruba*, acquired through his doctoral work on it, and his familiarity with the best of modern literature, both seem to have contributed in equal measure to the evolution of his unique narrative style.

To these formal elements, Rahi added a popular cultural dimension whose novelty still continues to shock. What the early critics of *Adha Gaon* were offended by, first and foremost, was the liberal use throughout the text of four-letter words, as frequently and routinely uttered by Rahi's rural subaltern characters. While no one can actually deny that in common everyday speech in Hindi a word such as *behanchod* (sister-fucker) or *gaandu* (bugger) comes trippingly off the tongue of a consider-able number of (especially lower-class) speakers almost as *a takiya-kalam* (an unthinking, meaningless filler), there has been a self-censoring consen-sus not to register and represent it in literature. Then came Rahi and broke the taboo in a manner no less radical than, say, that of James Joyce in *Ulysses* (1922).

His primary justification for doing so, Rahi said, was that he was merely putting down what his characters spoke, his practice in this regard being nothing if not authentic. With characteristic wit, he explained: 'If my characters speak in the language of the Bhagvadgita, I'll put down *shlokas* from the Gita, and if they speak in a string of four-letter words I'll put down four-letter words.' But authenticity here is not a mere matter of verisimilitude, for it also serves to deepen the emotion and its signifi-cance. Protesting against the injustice of poor Muslims today having to suffer for what their conquering forbearers may have done centuries ago, a character in *Adha Gaon* says: 'So, it was an emperor who smashed a temple, and it's we who get buggered for it.' It is difficult to replace the supposedly offending word here with some euphemism without taking away from the justness of the protest, and perhaps this was what Rahi meant when he said in the preface to *Topi Shukla* (a book which is remarkably free of four-letter words, perhaps on the rebound from the scandal caused by *Adha Gaon*) that perhaps the whole of this novel was a '*gandi gaali*', a filthy obscenity, and that he was uttering it from rooftops: 'This novel is obscene—like life itself.'

POETRY AND PROSE: URDU AND HINDI

Another, perhaps even more significant, aspect of Rahi's sensibility and style was that he was both a poet and a novelist, having started out as a poet in Urdu before he turned to writing novels in Hindi. There have, of course, been a number of other poet-novelists in various languages of the world, but Rahi was probably unique in writing all his poetry in one language, Urdu, and all his fiction in another, Hindi. This may seem to suggest that Rahi was an acute example of a dissociation of sensibility caused by the split between these two languages, a case perhaps of certifiable linguistic schizophrenia. On the other hand, it could also demonstrate, as indeed Rahi meant it to, that these two languages, differ-ent and even opposed in name and history, were perhaps not so different after all and were equally apt alternative mediums for his undivided, harmonizing, and unified sensibility.

While the poetry Rahi continued to write in Urdu has an unmistakable Urdu tone and cadence and also partakes of the traditional stock of Urdu imagery, it is quite different in the register and diction it employs, which are much closer to Hindi than most of the Urdu poetry written before Rahi (with the exception possibly and partially of two poets, Nazir Akbarabadi and Firaq Gorakhpuri). The very pen-name he chose for himself, Rahi, is so short and simple as to be equally accessible to the speakers of both Urdu and Hindi, unlike some other famous pen-names of Urdu poets such as Zauq, Zafar, Ghalib, Faiz, or Firaq. Indeed, Rahi brought his pen-name even closer to Hindi when he addressed himself in the *maqta* (the last couplet) of some of his *ghazals*, intimately and playfully, as 'Rahiji', and in some of his verses he evoked a cultural landscape in a phraseology which was unknown to Urdu poetry before (except again in some *rubaiyat* by Firaq who, however, was a rare Hindu poet writing in Urdu):

> *Pehle to Rahi ji ghar jao, Ganga ji men nahao*
> *Phir vahin tat par chadar taan ke let raho so jao*

(Why don't you now go home, Rahi ji, and take a bath in Gangaji
And then lie down right there by the river, cover yourself with a sheet and sleep.)

Such was home for Rahi and such his dream of homecoming.

Through the example he himself set in his novels and poems as well as through his repeated public interventions, Rahi pleaded for Urdu and Hindi to be regarded as a common language, available equally to Hindus and Muslims. He mocked and exposed as a lie the idea, promoted during the separatist campaign for the creation of Pakistan, that Urdu was the language exclusively or mainly of the Muslims. In *Adha Gaon*, all the Muslims living in the village Gangauli are shown habitually to be speaking Bhojpuri, the local dialect of Hindi, the same as their Hindu neighbours do, and any Muslim departing from this practice is subjected to instant mockery. For example, a Muslim seated in a prime spot during the Moharram celebrations goes out for a moment, comes back to find his place taken by somebody else, and says indignantly in Urdu, 'Why are you sitting in my place?' Whereupon the other person smiles and retorts in Bhojpuri, 'But why are you speaking in Urdu?'—as if that were unquestionably the greater transgression.

Not only did Rahi put Urdu in its place but he also took a more radical step—to go boldly where no Urdu writer had gone before. In the larger cause of Hindi-Urdu/Hindu-Muslim harmony, he argued that the two languages could really come closer together if Urdu shed its Perso-Arabic script and came to be written in the Devanagari script in which Hindi is written. This, incidentally, is just what has been happening over the past several decades when editions of a large number of Urdu poets, and of some novels too, have been published in the Devanagari script with footnotes provided at the bottom of the page to explain the more difficult words. Thus reclothed, even Ghalib for example has had many more editions published in the last few decades in Hindi/Devanagari than in Urdu/*rasmulkhat*.

Rahi's suggestion, however, won little assent among Urdu-speakers, many of whom in fact considered it as sacrilege. But Rahi had already been practising what he preached, and was speaking out of personal experience and conviction. Not many Hindi readers may know that his *Adha Gaon*, in which the characters speak in Bhojpuri and the narrator uses a language which is no more Urdu than Hindi, was actually written in the Urdu, i.e. Perso-Arabic script, before it was submitted to a Hindi publisher, Rajendra Yadav of Akshar Prakashan, who is himself a writer of fiction in Hindi, and then was edited by another Hindi writer, Kamaleshwar. *Adha Gaon*, written originally in the Urdu script, was first published in Hindi (1966) and was not published in the Urdu script until the year 2003, almost four decades after its first publication in Hindi! (Incidentally, this Urdu-script edition was launched at a ceremony held in Rahi's village Gangauli, by the same political leader, Pabbar Ram, whom he had decades ago helped win an election against his father.) For a parallel to this publishing phenomenon, we have to go back to Premchand, whose fifth novel, *Bazaar-e-Husn*, remained unpublished in Urdu until 1924 while it was snapped up for publication in its Hindi version under the widely different title *Seva-sadan* in 1919, or perhaps to Salman Rushdie, whose epoch-making book *Midnight's Children* was published in English in 1981 and in translation into all the major languages of the world shortly afterwards, but not in Hindi until 1997.

In his own practice and career, Rahi thus had bridged the gulf between Urdu and Hindi not only by writing in a common diction and idiom but also by the bold expedient of erasing the barrier between the two scripts. As if this was not enough, he went one step further to put under interrogation yet another determinedly distinctive aspect of Urdu vis-à-vis Hindi, which is the correct enunciation or pronunciation, known as *talaffuz*, especially of certain consonants which are peculiar to Urdu/ Arabic/Persian and which Hindi-speakers find difficult to duplicate. Nowhere is this issue problematized with such comic relish as in *Topi Shukla*, the novel in which Rahi boldly took it upon himself to spell out many of the major cultural and political differences that stand between Muslims and Hindus and serve to divide them.

TOPI SHUKLA

Topi Shukla is all about friendship between a Muslim and a Hindu character, and the great strength of the novel is that this friendship is portrayed not in a glibly idealistic or sentimental manner but warts and all, with a gritty feel of the various religious, cultural, political, economic, and even linguistic factors which stand in the way of such a friendship and threaten to undermine it. It is not an incidental or minor but a full-length and full-frontal friendship, with the two characters being each other's closest friends in the face of wide social disapproval and derision. A friendship such as this, which constitutes the central theme of the novel, is hardly to be found anywhere else in all of Hindi or Urdu literature.

The significance of such a friendship is sought to be highlighted by Rahi through his choosing to locate it not in any old place but in Aligarh, and particularly, in the Aligarh Muslim University. This town and institution have long been regarded as a 'citadel of Muslim communalism' (as Rahi puts it without mincing words in this novel), ever since Sir Syed Ahmed Khan made it the centre of his movement to modernize and revitalize the Muslim community and to reconcile it better to the British rulers who apparently harboured a lingering distrust of all Muslims following the Mutiny of 1857. In the first half of the twentieth century, Aligarh came to be known as the intellectual hotbed of the separatist movement for Pakistan; in *Adha Gaon*, it is university students from Aligarh who are shown to visit Gangauli to try and convert the villagers to the new creed of Pakistan.

It is in such a setting and ambience that Topi and Iffan conduct their friendship, and therefore, besides Topi himself, almost every character of any significance in this novel is understandably a Muslim. But Rahi raises the stakes even higher by making Topi not only a dear friend of Iffan's but an equally dear and cherished friend of his wife Sakeena, a relationship which is predictably misunderstood and slandered all around. This is almost as bold and potentially explosive a device of the plot in this novel as was the friendship between Adela Quested and Dr Aziz in *A Passage to India*; the heroine in both stories is believed to be, as it were, a pawn captured by the other side.

Topi and Iffan are united not only by their personal affinity but also by a common enemy. This is communalism, the widespread assumption that Hindus and Muslims cannot possibly be, and probably shouldn't be, friends at all. Such benighted opposition, of course, further cements the bond between Topi and Iffan. But both of them have another enemy as well, and it is wholly consistent with Rahi's materialist progressive vision that this other major issue in the novel should have been conceived by him in stark economic terms. The bottom-line in the novel is that Topi is looking for a job and Iffan is looking for a promotion in his job, and the odds are stacked against each of them, not only because of a communalist bias but also because of a university system which plays a politics of its own in which merit is often the first thing to be sacrificed. As in *Adha Gaon* so in *Topi Shukla*, the ultimate question, in Rahi's Marxist understanding, is not religious or cultural but economic; as Iffan explicitly states towards the end of the novel: 'It is not a question of Hindi and Urdu or of Hindu and Mussalman. . . . It's a question of employment [*naukri*].' Though it is not anywhere developed in the novel, the ideological assumption here is that in a society where everyone's economic needs are adequately looked after, all other causes of conflict will just wither away.

Meanwhile, all kinds of factors which may serve to prevent or impede friendship between Muslims and Hindus are seemingly given free play in *Topi Shukla*. It is a major part of Rahi's strength and distinctiveness as a novelist that even on as 'sensitive' an issue as Hindu-Muslim relationships, he has the courage to explicitly identify and name all the prejudices that poison such relationships. He is the opposite of being mealymouthed; in fact, part of the thrill of reading him is that he goes along calling each spade not only a spade but (given his frankness of language) a bloody shovel. Such open naming of prejudices, suspicions, and fears may possibly result—and perhaps in real life does often result— in further aggravation and conflict, but in artistic representation, such dramatic, and even accentuated, confrontation leads paradoxically to what Aristotle called catharsis—a purging of the emotions and sentiments which are too irrational and overpowering for us to handle without artistic mediation.

For example, the first time Iffan brings *Topi Shukla* home and introduces him to his wife Sakeena ('This is my childhood friend Balbhadra Narayan Shukla'), she promptly says to him: 'Couldn't you have chosen a simpler name?' Iffan next informs Sakeena that Topi does not eat anything touched by a Muslim, and she says: 'That's good news, for as it happens we have nothing at the moment fit for a yokel.' Of course, Topi now proceeds to have his first meal in a Muslim household, but then he tells Sakeena, 'Don't ever ask me to eat with you again,' for he still is, he claims, a dyed-in-the-wool Hindu. Whereupon Sakeena retorts that she is no less of a dyed-in-the-wool Muslim, and when Topi leaves, she will have the plates scrubbed thoroughly clean. Topi now is allowed the last word: 'Or else you wouldn't have had them washed at all perhaps? You filthy

Muslims.' These mounting insults and counter-insults cause in the reader a *frisson* such as he may seldom have experienced before so far as Hindu-Muslim interaction is concerned, either in literature or in life; the kid gloves are off, the knives are out, and this, finally, is for real. This scene is a prime example of Rahi's belief that it is only by acknowledging and expressing our worst prejudices that we shall ever be able to expurgate them.

Perhaps the most sustained play of such a prejudice in *Topi Shukla* concerns Urdu and Hindi, the long-running joke here being that Topi is shown to be congenitally challenged so far as correct pronunciation of Urdu words is concerned, of getting his *sheen-qaaf* right, as the phrase goes. Sheen-qaaf in Urdu denotes the correct pronunciation of certain Urdu consonants (such as qaaf though not quite sheen) which do not occur in indigenous words in Hindi or in most other Indian languages. A basic example occurs early in the novel when Topi in an over-compensatory effort says *fir* for *phir*. (Incidentally, this difference cannot be represented in the roman script in which 'f' and 'ph' are pronounced the same way.) After Iffan has pointed this out to Topi, he on the rebound makes the opposite error of saying '*pharaq*' for '*faraq*', and thus he stumbles through the novel, saying 'k' for 'q' and the other way round (and the roman script fails once again to distinguish between these two sounds) or 's' for 'sh'.

This marks Topi out as an illiterate laughing-stock or worse, he is shown to be a Hindi bull in the Urdu china shop. Moreover, both Iffan and Sakeena mock with the same sense of superiority any Hindi that Topi may use which they themselves cannot cope with, for example the way he pronounces the retroflex 'n', as in '*kaaran*' or '*Ravana*' (a sound which, like several others, Urdu-speakers in their turn cannot produce), or his use of words like *yadi* and *parantu* which Sakeena forbids him to use after she has mimicked them as 'your *yadi-padi*' and '*arantu-parantu*'. On her part, she cannot, and would not, throughout the novel learn to pronounce either Topi's proper name or his father's (Bhrigu Narayan), as if it wasn't worth the bother and indeed their own fault. Perhaps the most remarkable instance of such linguistic *hauteur* occurs when Sakeena mocks the word *pragatisheel* as '*aragati-paragati-sheel* or whatever', and then says of Hindi: 'What kind of a wretched language is it that when you speak it, your tongue goes twisting and twirling a hundred different ways, like a sluttish woman.' This is rich, particularly coming from a woman.

Such superiority of Urdu and the Muslims over Hindi and the Hindus is flaunted in the face of Topi by his two closest friends in the novel, Iffan and Sakeena, notwithstanding the greatest goodwill between them. It is part of Rahi's subtle and insidious art that as the novel progresses and such examples multiply, and as Topi keeps protesting that Iffan and Sakeena should pay attention to what he is saying rather than how he is saying it, the reader begins to realize that an implicit faith in the refined superiority of Urdu over Hindi is, in fact, yet another example of Muslim arrogance and chauvinism, which even Iffan and Sakeena, for all their liberalism and enlightenment, cannot bring themselves to question. It is especially apt that Rahi should weave such residual prejudice into the texture of the novel by thematizing the very use of the language, so that the medium and the message are intertwined and language is made to expose language as the last test of our capacity for tolerance and harmony. (Incidentally, to spare a thought for the usually unsung translator, such thorny Urdu-Hindu negotiation in this novel must have made the rendering of this novel into English particularly challenging.)

RAHI'S ACHIEVEMENT

It has been claimed that Rahi Masoom Raza belongs to the line of Kabir, Rasakhan (the seventeenth century Muslim poet who composed some of the sweetest Hindi verses ever written on Lord Krishna), Rahim (Akbar's courtier who wrote verses in Hindi as well as Sanskrit), and Premchand, and there is no doubt that he belongs to the sturdy secular tradition of Hindi writers who spanned religions or languages or both. But he also has a unique and pioneering place of his own in the history of contemporary Hindi literature, for he was the first Muslim writer of any significance to write in Hindi rather than in Urdu ever since Urdu emerged as an alternative language of literary expression nearly two hundred years ago. It was only after Partition (and in some unfortunate ways the vindication with it of the separatist claim that Urdu was an essential marker of Muslim identity) that several Muslim writers who had decided to stay back in India returned to Hindi in a big way, and Rahi's radical example has been followed by a number of younger Muslim novelists, notably Gulrez Khan Shani, Asghar Wajahat, Abdul Bismillah, and Manzoor Ehtesham.

Rahi and these other novelists have in their works admitted us into Muslim society and Muslim households for the first time since the rise of the novel in Hindi. It is not that Hindu novelists did not depict Muslim characters in their works, but as Rahi himself asserted in his review of a novel by Kamaleshwar which he praised highly enough, a Hindu novelist cannot help the reader cross the threshold of a Muslim household and show what lies behind the curtain and the veil. Topi says in one of his no-holds-barred arguments with Iffan: 'Every Muslim [in India] has a little hatch which opens onto Pakistan'; it was Rahi's path-breaking achievement to open a hatch for the Hindi reader onto the intimacy and interiority of Indian Muslim life. Nor was the view thus revealed entirely rosy for, to Rahi's credit, his insider depiction of Muslim life is not a romanticized celebration but rather a heartfelt and often anguished excoriation.

And yet, it must be admitted that Rahi's actual literary achievement falls somewhat short of his grand imaginative and ideological project. As *Topi Shukla* amply demonstrates, Rahi was perhaps a little too schematic and peremptory in his plotting and characterization, a little too arbitrary and improvisatory as a *qissago* narrator, a little too obvious and assertive in his self-appointed role as an intrusive commentator, a little too narrow and mechanically materialistic in his analysis of the causes of his one running theme—Muslim-Hindu relations—and altogether, a little too prompt and forthcoming with his secular pieties. He was perhaps more of a fighter in a noble cause than an accomplished artist; he had, as he himself would have readily and happily admitted, always a palpable design on us readers.

But Rahi's heart was clearly in the right place, and his vision of our postcolonial nation was bold, worthy, and laudable. He dedicated one of his novels, as he put it, to his three mothers: Nafisa Begum, the Aligarh Muslim University, and the river Ganga (and this sounds no more like a fable than some of the strange ways in which some characters are born in the Mahabharat!). One could add that, with such multicultural conception and birth, he sought to embody and incarnate in himself the secular Indian nation. In his own simple but original description, he was a 'Hindu Mussalman'.

As a writer, he adopted as his grand theme an issue, communalism, whose crucial importance for the well-being of our body politic has only grown with the passage of time, and his treatment of it was uncompromising and unflinching. He was not a sugary dream-merchant; rather, he alternated only too plausibly between hope and despair. At the end of this novel, Topi Shukla feels defeated and commits suicide, and Rahi himself often experienced a profound liberal gloom and sense of failure. In one of his best-known couplets, he said:

> *Larte larte haar gaye hum*
> *Lagta hai bekaar gaye hum.*

(I fought the good fight again and again
And lost. Did I live my life in vain?)

The answer must, of course, be a resounding no, for works such as *Adha Gaon* and *Topi Shukla* will continue to stimulate and sensitize all of us who read them, enabling us to appreciate better many vital issues and aspects of our national life, and perhaps also to carry on fighting the good fight each in our own way.

Delhi   HARISH TRIVEDI
October 2004

I

'... So, brother, do you now see how politics enters religion?' said Topi, concluding his speech.

'No,' said Iffan. While Topi was expounding his thesis, Iffan's thoughts were elsewhere. You see, there are issues greater than religion and politics—issues like domestic problems. And one has time to think of these problems only when a friend is making a speech as if to a surging sea of humanity whereas you are, in fact, the only listener!

Iffan's reply dampened Topi.

'Just explain that again.' Iffan goaded him.

'See, there's this Dharma Samaj College?'

'Yes.'

'This belongs to the Agarwal *baniyas*.'

'Yes,' agreed Iffan.

'And *Barahseni* belongs to the Barahsenis.'

'Yes.'

'You know, these Barahsenis have quite a unique story.'

'And what's their story?'

'Their original name in its pure form was *Duvadas Shreni*. They soon realized that this Sanskrit name would not work here so they promptly translated it into Hindi. And the baniyas of Duvadas Shreni became the Barahseni baniyas. And now these people do not even remember what their name had been during the Mughal regime.'

'They have done nothing great by changing Shreni into Seni,' said Iffan. 'This is an absolutely incorrect translation.'

'This was not translated by a professor or some great great scholar or some grammarian.' Topi began to get angry. 'This was done by ordinary people. And ordinary people have no time to ponder over the niceties of grammar. They cut and shape words according to the measure of their knowledge of language.'

'But *seni*? Food comes in a seni,' continued Iffan.

'Maybe it does.' Topi was upset. 'But Shreni did get converted into Seni.' He said this, grinding his teeth. There wasn't really any serious provocation for him to do this grinding bit but Topi, you see, was excessively fond of his sparkling white teeth. That is why he would show them off even if the occasion did not warrant it. Deep dark complexion. Teeth as white as snow. He was his own negative, waiting perhaps for his print to be developed.

Topi's full name was Balbhadra Narayan Shukla. His father's name was even more difficult. His grandfather's name—well, even Topi could not recall it correctly. But whenever Iffan would say to him: 'Topi—*yaar*, no respectable person can get your name right,' Topi would reply: 'Maybe not a respectable Urdu gentleman, brother. But a respectable Hindu will surely be able to get this right. And who would think that your name is simple? Sayyed Jargaam Murtaja Abadi. *Wah*! I know I haven't pronounced your name correctly, but you see I don't speak Urdu.'

This reply would always silence Iffan. And it would become clear that in these days no one was just *shareef*, respectable. Every shareef person had a prefix attached—Hindu shareef, Muslim shareef, Urdu shareef, Hindi shareef—and of course, there is Bihar Sharif! The jungle of respectable people seems to have spread far and wide. Iffan would always be saddened by this thought. But I'm not here to tell you Iffan's sad story. We were talking about Topi. I have already told you that his name was Balbhadra Narayan Shukla. But people called him Topi Shukla.

This was because the Aligarh University that is famous for *Matti, Makkhi, Matthri, Makkhan,* and *Maulvis,* is also well-known for the various new names it gave to people. One person was called Qa. Another was called Ustaad Chuvaara. (Perhaps these weren't distributed during some *Nikaah* ceremony!) One was called Iqbal Headache. Then there was Scoundrel Iqbal. Another was Conceited Iqbal. And one Iqbal was called Iqbal Nothing. Nothing because all other Iqbals had some name or the other attached to theirs. And if no name were attached to his name, he would feel bad. So he began to be called Iqbal Nothing. There was a Geography teacher called Behrul Kaahil. This teacher could never do any work fast and *kaahil* means sluggish. And so he was called the Kaahili Sea (in the Arabic language the Pacific Ocean is called Behrul Kaahil)! Another Geography teacher was called Cigar Hussain Zaidi as he was, at one time, passionately fond of cigars. . . . Balbhadra Narayan Shukla was one more link in this chain. He was christened Topi.

At the University Union meetings, there was a tradition that one could not make a speech without covering one's head. Topi was adamant that he would not wear a *topi* to cover his head. So what would usually happen was that whenever he would stand up to speak, the entire Union hall would reverberate with cries of 'Topi! Topi!' Gradually, the relationship between Balbhadra Narayan and Topi deepened. As a result, Balbhadra was abandoned and Topi Shukla remained. Soon, close friends discarded the impeding word Shukla. And he became, simply, Topi.

But one day Topi did something radical. It was the budget session of the Union. He wished to raise a few objections. He pulled off the topi from his neighbour's head, put it on his own and stood up to speak. (The topi was too large for his head.) When the boys saw him with a topi on his head, they were greatly upset.

'This is betrayal,' said a voice from behind.

As soon as he started speaking, the boys screamed that he should take off his topi. Ultimately he had to take it off. And when he removed his topi and stood bare-headed, they went back to their usual chanting of 'Topi, Topi'. He had to don it on again, and it was only then that the boys became quiet and allowed him to speak. They however liked this antic of his so much that they agreed to pass whatever amendment he wished to suggest in the budget.

Topi Shukla was a friendly sort of person. And very principled. One of his staunchest principles was that no principles could be allowed to impede friendship. When he came to the University, he belonged with the Jana Sangh. Slowly, he became part of the Muslim League. As a result the Hindu boys started calling him *Maulana* Topi.

If there were ever a riot in Aligarh, he would not go to the other side of the Wooden Bridge for fear that he would be mistaken for a Muslim and murdered.

Had done his M.A. in Hindi. Was unemployed.

There was a vacancy in the Hindi department in some D.A.V. College. Iffan took a cutting of the advertisement from the paper, presented it to Topi and said: 'Apply.'

Our man said, 'What's the use *Bhai*.'

Iffan said, 'C'mon, you'll have a job, what else?'

Our man: 'This is a Hindu college. I won't get a job here.'

'Then apply to some Muslim College,' said Iffan bitterly.

But Topi was not willing to do this either. He said: 'My name is Balbhadra Narayan Shukla.'

This leads us to an important question—Is there any place in this country for people like Balbhadra Narayan Shukla and for his counterpart—say someone with a name like Anwar Hussain? Here there is more or less enough space for grocers, butchers, Sayyeds, Julahas, Rajputs, Muslim Rajputs, Barahsenis, Agarwals, Kayasths, Christians, Sikhs . . . but where is the place for an Indian? It is quite possible that honest people have become Hindus and Muslims because of unemployment.

'This bloody politics has invaded religion too,' Topi said angrily.

'Religion has always been a form of politics. You cannot build the Somnath Temple nor can I build the Jama Masjid. Then why will religion support you or me, silly?'

'I think I should get married,' said Topi.

Iffan was completely taken by surprise because Topi's wedding plans were hardly anywhere near Iffan's thoughts.

'You think you should—do that?'

'I am not joking,' said Topi. 'This seems to be the only solution to my problems. Just let me get married and *fir* (then) I'll show you how I tackle this bloody world.'

'The word is not fir. It's *phir*.'

'Hardly makes any *pharaq* (difference).'

'*Faraq*, not pharaq.'

'That's it—you people just go about licking the soles of words.' Topi was annoyed. 'Here I am, talking about my marriage plans and you are immersed in your language improvement programme.'

'But who is it that you wish to marry?'

'Would I be here talking with you if I had the answer to this question?' Topi was getting really angry now. 'You know Bhai, sometimes you say such stupid things.'

'Really, now, what do you want me to do? Produce a female child for you?'

'How will that help?' said Topi. 'You know I cannot marry your child.'

'So?' asked Iffan.

'Just arrange my affair with someone.'

'Arrange an affair?'

'Yes.'

'And why should I myself not have an affair with the person I arrange for you?'

'Ay, listen Bhai, I warn you, don't you dare talk rubbish. You want to have an affair when you are already married?'

'Look here, *Pandit* Balbhadra Narayan Topi Shukla. There is no dearth of girls with whom affairs may be fixed or with whom it could be arranged for you to fall in love. But it is not necessary that the girl who loves you will eventually marry you. Love is associated with the heart. Marriage, with your salary. The kind of wife you get will depend on the kind of money you earn.'

'Does this mean that the stories of *Laila Majnu* and *Heer Ranjha* are mere fiction?'

'These stories existed before the middle class was born,' said Iffan.

'This means that this bloody politics has entered the realm of *ishq* (love) too. I said ishq correctly, na?'

'I suggest that you stick to your language.'

'Fir you will complain that I am ruining my mother tongue.'

'No,' said Iffan. 'Phir I will make no complaints.'

'Fir why don't you fix an affair for me? And if you can fix it with a Muslim girl, I'd be delighted.'

'Why?'

'I'll take her and migrate to Pakistan. By the way, would you have three rupees?'

'Rupees?' Iffan was taken aback.

'Yes, yes. Rupees.'

'What will you do with the money?'

'Yaar, Bhai, you have become very dull,' Topi condoled. 'I'll spend the money, what else.'

'Ay, Topi!' That was Iffan's wife, Sakeena. 'Have dinner here before you go.'

'Ram Ram Ram.' Topi stood up. '*Bhabi*, you are bent upon corrupting my religion, aren't you? How many times do I have to tell you that I do not eat in a Muslim's house?'

'Why don't you?' Iffan got angry. 'You claim to be a progressive sort, don't you?'

'Yes, I do. But there's something called habit,' said Topi. 'Even now, when I go home I am not allowed to enter into the kitchen. My mother keeps a separate plate for me. Says I have been polluted. But you know how it is—she is my mother. Occasionally, she does shower her love upon me. And then she goes straight to the Ganga to have a bath. One day I told her, 'Mother, these Muslims have polluted Gangaji by bathing there all the time.' Believe me, she was so angry that she did not speak to me for six months.'

'And your father?' Sakeena drew up her sleeves, sat on the arm of Iffan's chair, wiping her forehead with her *dupatta*.

Iffan shut his pen. He knew now that he would not be able to work for hours.

Sakeena and Topi were great friends. But the two could not get along for even a minute. Sakeena was perpetually angry with the Hindus because her family members had been killed during the partition riots.

'Topi,' she said, 'I know you people only too well. God knows how you can sit here and say that you are some "essive" or the other . . .'

'Progressive,' Topi helped her out.

'Yes, yes, I know that. Some "argessive pergessive" or the other. Allah! —What kind of a blessed language is this? When you speak it, your tongue goes twirling and twisting like a slut.'

'Why are you wasting these similes? What is it that you want to say? Why don't you say it directly?'

'*Arre*, you think I'm scared of you that I will not say what I want to?' Sakeena got up from the arm of the chair. 'I was saying that you sit here and talk of being pergessive but beneath the skin you too are a Hindu.'

'There. Now when did I ever say that I have become a Muslim? Am I mad to abandon a majority community and become part of a minority community?'

'You are a Janasanghi spy.'

'But at this moment what I'm looking for is three rupees.'

'I don't have three rupees.'

'Would you have five?'

'And why not? Hadn't your father, some god-knows-what Narayan Shukla, planted a money tree in my garden? This year it has been in full bloom.'

'Amazing. My father never mentioned this to me.'

'It is not so amazing that you have to say that it is amazing,' said Iffan. Sakeena could not control her laughter. She pulled out a five-rupee note tied to the end of her dupatta and extended it towards Topi.

'Take this. But as soon as you get a job, return the amount.'

'Have written it down, Bhabi,' said Topi, getting up to go. 'I shall pay back every borrowed penny with interest. And look here, when you run out of money completely, just get me a job somewhere please, ok?'

Before Sakeena could think of a fitting reply, Topi left.

This is the Balbhadra Narayan Shukla who is the hero of this story.

One of the methods of narrating a story or a biography is for the story-teller or the biographer to start the story or biography at any point. Just like life, the beginning of a story too is not very significant. Only the ending is significant. The end of life and the end of a story. If I had begun by showing you how Balbhadra Narayan Shukla lay in a cot like a piece of blackened meat, bawling, that he had a waist-chain of black thread and on his black forehead was placed a black *kaajal* mark—it is quite possible that you would have turned your face wondering what could be special about this child!

However, the truth is that every story and every biography begins exactly like this.

II

Like all the ordinary and not-so-ordinary people of the world, Topi too was born without a name. Only those who die need to have a name. Gandhi too was born nameless, and so was Godse. To date, no one has been required to have a name in order to be born. At the time of birth everyone is only a child. By the time they die they become Hindu, Muslim, Christian, atheist, Indian, Pakistani, White, Black, and so many such more.

There is no point in quibbling over these things at this juncture. Now it is enough for us to know just this that Topi was born. Like thousands and lakhs and crores of second sons he too was a second son. There was one brother older than him and he was older than another brother.

The night Topi was born was a wretched, dark, rainy night. There was absolutely no breeze. The sky, densely packed with clouds, held no space for even a star.

Just as his mother felt the first pains, a bar of lightning struck the sky. There was a crack in the clouds. A sheet of water started pouring down. It seemed as if the clouds were trapped in the eaves of a thatching.

The courtyard glistened with droplets of water. All of a sudden the lights went off. Darkness was complete. His grandmother began to chant 'Hare Krishna Hare Krishna', wondering what demon was to be born that created such darkness to surround its birth. His father, Dr Bhrugu Narayan Shukla of the Blue Oil, too, was quite anxious. On this stormy night neither a midwife nor a lady doctor would be able to come.

After a point it became imperative for Pandit Balbhadra Narayan Shukla to be born, alone, exactly at midnight. As soon as Topi was born, he saw the world with his tiny eyes. What he saw was extremely frightening. Scared, he began to cry and started searching for the darkness in which he had floated happily till some time ago. The wheels of history and time, however, do not move backwards. Topi had to enter into this world despite the fact that the outside radiance was quite killing. This is the reason why the old and wise women never allowed light or air to enter into the room where a woman was to give birth. (Even today this practice is maintained in those places where the wise and old women continue to hold sway.)

That Eve gave Adam wheat to eat and because of this blunder they were thrown out of Paradise is an absolutely wrong story. That tree in paradise is not even a tree of lust as portrayed by psychologists. That was a tree of light. Slavery, religion, and light have been perpetual antagonists. When Adam got a beam of light, God immediately threw him out of Paradise.

This tree of light can be seen in several old stories as well. Scholars and astrologers made calculations and said that the Prince was quite lucky but that for fourteen years he should remain untouched by even the reflections of the sun and the moon. What then? A beautiful dome was made which was covered by a huge canopy. The Prince with his retinue of special concubines, women from the harem, water bearers, some important and some unimportant people—in short, with all the paraphernalia and grandeur of the palace, was sent to live in this dome-like cupola. One day (when the fourteenth year was nearing completion), the Prince saw a bright thing growing from the ceiling to the ground. This tree, which was upside-down, was nothing but the tree of light. The light had pierced a hole in the tent. Well . . . as soon as the Prince saw the tree of light he was besotted with trouble. Nature manifested itself as the supernatural and a child growing in an unnatural environment had to confront the real world. The Prince had to face a lot of troubles, but he did not let the light he held in his hands slip by. In the end, the Prince married the lady he loved and that was the end of the story.

This could quite possibly be Adam's story as well. The tent propped up in Paradise may have developed a hole. . . . The old Emperor is still waiting for the Prince, for the story is not over yet. The Prince is even now searching for a way out, caught as he is in the jungle of Doctor Ward and hydrogen bombs, the blacks and whites, and Hindu-Muslim riots.

But our Balbhadra Narayan Shukla was neither Adam nor the Prince. That is why he was not scared of either the demons or the astrologers. He was merely the second son of Pandit Bhrugu Narayan Shukla of the Blue Oil and in this word, 'merely', lay the tragedy of Topi's life. To tell you the truth, this story is just about this 'being merely'.

Doctor Pandit Bhrugu Narayan of the Blue Oil was a very good man, in the opinion of the people in the neighbourhood. A very religious person. Often went to the temple. Did *pooja* occasionally. Had built a very beautiful temple in the city. He had just one hobby—to contest elections. Always lost them but never lost courage and stood again to contest every election. He first stood as a Congress candidate. Lost. Independent candidate. Lost. As a Janasangh candidate. Lost. He stood for every election—from the Parliamentary to the Municipal elections—and lost. Now you tell me, where can you find such large-hearted losers!

Doctor Saheb adored the Persian language and was crazy about Masanvi Maulana Room. Would often hum verses from *Urf* and *Bedil*. Would speak a diluted version of Urdu and was a staunch opponent of that language. Would never say anything less worthy than *Insha allah, Maasha allah, Subahan allah*. Hated Muslims. Not because they had destroyed the ancient Indian culture and created Pakistan. But because he had to contest elections against Doctor Sheikh Sharfuddin of the Red Oil. This Doctor Sheikh Sharfuddin used to be his compounder once upon a time and his sons used to call him Sharfu *Chacha*. What Sheikh Sharfuddin did was simple—he changed the colour of the Blue Oil. Just that. He changed the colour of the oil and became a doctor and started looting the innocent masses rather liberally. How people change when the colours change! The topi is just one. But if it is a white one, the wearer looks like a Congress-man; if it is red, then like a Socialist; if saffron, then like a Jansanghi.

Despite this, Doctor Bhrugu Narayan's business was a roaring success. The Blue Oil brought life to muscles and bones. And the youth these days generally suffer from weak muscle toning. The Blue Oil would tone up the flaccid muscles and make them firm and sharp as a sword. (Incidentally, this is what the Red Oil did too!) That is why Doctor Bhrugu Narayan, by the grace of Allah or God, had, in his house, a wife, four maids, two male servants, one buffalo, two Alsatian dogs, one car, and three children.

Babu Bhrugu Narayan, however, is not the hero of this story. I have introduced Doctor Saheb to you because without knowing him, it is difficult to get a proper perspective of the personality of Pandit Balbhadra Narayan Topi Shukla.

Topi's mother, Ramdulari, was a simple, home-loving, religious type of woman. His elder brother, Muneshwar Narayan Shukla, alias Munni Babu, could be spotted in every nook and corner of the Ramrajya constituency. And Topi's younger brother, Bhairav Narayan, was fond of becoming a Congressman because he had learnt that in this profession the chances of making quick money were greater than he could ever hope to make by selling Blue Oil. Whenever he heard of a chief minister of some state having passed away and having left behind fifty lakh of rupees in a Swiss bank, or of a chief minister who used to be a bus conductor before he became chief minister and was now the owner of several palatial mansions in every big city in this country and owned several mills, his eyes would sparkle and he would push himself onto his mother Ramdulari's lap and say: 'I will become a Chief Minister.'

Ramdulari would say: 'The Great God has miraculous powers. I'm sure you will become CM one day.' Hearing this Bhairav would be convinced that he would become a Chief Minister one day or the other. But he could never speak about his desires to his father. He was the youngest, so he was his mother's favourite.

Doctor Saheb, however, was sold on his eldest son, Munni Babu, and Munni Babu was sold on Munnibai.

Munni Babu had fallen for Munnibai's coy ways—a charm he could not resist. Well, like the other hundred odd prostitutes in the city, she too was a prostitute. But Munnibai had not given up her religious ways even though she was in this profession. She knew that one day she would have to face God. And so she had kept a Shivling in one of the rooms in her house. Every morning, she would bathe and perform a pooja for Nataraj, Bhole Shankar, Bhoothnath. And in the evenings, when she would deck herself with all her thirty-two armours and open shop, she would take care to see that no matter what song reached her ears, it should be devoid of obscenity. She was very upset by the fact that it was a Musalman who had robbed her of her virginity. And this was precisely the attribute that Munni Babu found irresistible. He was ten years younger than Munnibai. But does age count in matters of the heart?

This was the reason why when talk of Munni Babu's marriage started circulating, he became forlorn. And not just that he hung his head in despair, he also refused to get married. Doctor Saheb was very worried because the bride's family was a very good catch. One lakh in cash. One car. Five *sers* of gold. 30 sers of silver. . . . Doctor Saheb analysed the pros and cons of this situation and decided to explain matters to Munni Babu. But who could explain things to him better than Munnibai? For five thousand rupees Munnibai agreed to help him put things in the right perspective. She went off to Bombay for a year. Doctor Saheb also sent her a letter through one of his patients (his patient became a hero); but when Munnibai vanished without leaving word behind, Munni Babu did as he was told by his father.

Munni Babu was married off to Lajvanti, the only daughter of Pandit Sudhakar Laal.

Lajvanti was a very nice girl. Except that she had one bad eye. She dragged her left foot while walking. Her complexion was slightly concealed. And her face had puck marks. But how can these things be important? Do respectable people ever bother about the looks of daughters-in-law? Good looks are meant for prostitutes. It is important for a wife to have good health. Lajvanti had both—good health and a good temperament. In short, she was the only daughter of Pandit Sudhakar Laal. Panditji was the best-known lawyer in the city. Had an income of around ten to twelve thousand. Was a big landlord. Was a partner in several businesses. His father had been a powerful policeman in his days. And grandfather had been an even more powerful *tehsildar*. It was generally said that in Panditji's house currency notes were kept out in the sun to dry the way foodgrains are kept. Father and grandfather had left behind a bank balance of seventeen lakhs apart from the hundred and fifty shops and five palatial homes. But Lajvanti was not a ruined case that the lawyer could salvage. Hers was a ruined face! They could not get her a groom from among equals. Those belonging to a lesser class too did not wish to sacrifice their sons to an ugly statue of Lakshmi. They could find only one Pandit Bhrugu Narayan of the Blue Oil who believed that Lakshmi would always be Lakshmi.

Munni Babu's and Lajvanti's stories too are not part of Topi Shukla's story. Actually, I want all of you to have a look at all those people who stifle Topi from all sides.

However, I notice that this talk meanders. This talk of Munni Babu's and Lajvanti's marriage has cropped up quite unnecessarily. That's why we'll return to that dark rainy night when a child was born. The child who would later become Pandit Balbhadra Narayan Shukla and later still become Topi Shukla.

Topi Shukla had an ugly face. But he was very modest. He was not born naked. He let the hair on his head grow all over his body—and that's how he was born. As a result, when the servant came home in the morning and massaged Rumdulari and then left for her home, she told her husband: 'A chimpanzee's been born to *daagdar* saheb.'

Topi's entire family—from his mother's side and from his father's side—were plunged in a major state of confusion wondering who exactly it was that he took after. But there seemed to be no answer to this puzzle. What next? The mother-in-law's tongue started rolling. Poor Ramdulari— she wondered what mess she had got into by giving birth to this child. One of the only redeeming things about this whole issue was that whenever her mother-in-law got furious, she started speaking in Persian. And Ramdulari did not understand a word of what she said.

Subhadradevi, that is Doctor Bhrugu Narayan Shukla's mother, was an admirer of Phaarsi and hated Hindi. Her father, grandfather of the Blue Oil Doctor, Pandit Balmukund, was a Persian-Arabic scholar and an Urdu-Persian poet. Subhadra was his only daughter. He taught her Phaarsi to his heart's content. Subhadradevi even started writing couplets in Phaarsi on the sly. The family she was married into also encouraged the Phaarsi influence. Doctor Bhrugu's father was himself a lover of Urdu-Phaarsi. Whenever Subhadradevi wanted to say something that was not meant for the ears of her servants and orderlies, she would speak with her husband in Phaarsi. The husband and wife looked upon Hindi as the language of the illiterate.

Poor Ramdulari. She could not follow a word of the language her mother-in-law spoke. In her own house the tradition of education was different. But this much she most definitely understood—her mother-in-law was not too pleased with this newborn grandson. She glanced at her child with great trepidation. Even now he was ugly. And was looking at the ceiling with his very black and white eyes.

Ramdulari's spirit got sore with her mother-in-law's comments. Her heart became bitter. And perhaps because of this bitterness, her milk got bad. For some reason, she could not feed her child. She was fed almonds and milk, *halwa* and *laddoo*. Saints and beggars were appeased. Witchcraft was consulted. The feet of ascetics were touched. But her milk did not flow.

Topi Shukla's ugliness increased Munni Babu's market value. Whatever came into the house went first to Munni Babu. Clothes would be ordered for Munni Babu and Topi would wear those discarded by Munni Babu. Subhadradevi did not let him come anywhere near her. She probably feared that if she even barely touched Topi her golden coloured skin would be tarnished.

On the other hand, Munni Babu could sit forever on his *Daadi*'s lap. Daadi sometimes told him stories from *Gulistan*. Sometimes she took him around *Tilasm-e-Hoshruba*. At some times she told him the Ramayana and at other times she reminded him of the stories of the brave warriors of the Mahabharata.

Our Balbhadra, too, wished that someone would tell him stories so lovingly. But all around him, on all four sides, was intense silence. If he ever insisted on having something, he would be sternly admonished and told that he was shameless to be competing with his older brother.

What happened as a result was that he grew to hate the stories of Shekh Saadi, Ameer Hamza, the Ramayana, the Mahabharata—and all elders. He thought of all these as belonging to Munni Babu's party. And one day he crossed all limits. Told his Daadi: 'Daadiji, you pray to that dark god

Krishna na, see, one day, your prayers will all, *jaroor*, definitely, get blackened.'

That day Daadiji was angry on two counts. One was that her grandson pronounced '*zaroor*' as 'jaroor'. (Topi continued to deliberately mispronounce words throughout her life in order to annoy her.) And the other was that he had made fun of her God. She plucked her arrows of accusations and struck them straight into Ramdulari's heart. And that day, pouring out all her pent-up anger, Ramdulari scolded Topi.

Topi ran away from home.

III

It was not as if he had decided to run away without giving this act much thought. He thought as much as a six or a six-and-a-half year-old could think about this matter. For instance, he did think about food and about the problem of sleeping at night. But these were not serious problems at all, were they? I'll eat at home and sleep in my bed. He took a maximum of three to four seconds to make his mind up. That is why when people learnt that he had run away from home each one rebuked him for doing foolish things impetuously.

But I (that is this biographer) know that Topi Shukla never did anything impetuously. And this later on proved to be the tragedy of his life. These, however, are things that you will learn for yourself as we proceed with the Topi saga.

Anyway! So what happened that day was when Ramdulari lost all control and beat Topi in a temper, he thought of all the possible alternatives and only after that did he decide to run away from home. And if he hadn't run away then perhaps I would not have written this biography. This running away was a significant event in his life, because it was this act that led to his meeting with Iffan.

When Topi ran away from home, he left behind not just his house but also his neighbourhood. And on leaving his neighbourhood the first thing he saw was two boys beating up another. He knew enough arithmetic to understand that if one were added to one it would become two. So he added one to one.

By the time the fight was over his *kurta* was in shreds. The skin from his knees had peeled off. And nail marks had etched themselves on his face. Iffan too suffered a similar fate. But there was one difference between Iffan and Topi. Iffan was an only son while Topi was a 'middle' son. This issue may not appear to be very significant to you. But only those who are 'middle' sons can understand the pain and hurt of being one. If you really wish to know, then the truth is that I write this biography only for the sake of the second sons of the world so that they can benefit from this and, if possible, start an 'International Federation of Second Sons' and make a demand for their rights. If Blacks and Whites, Hindus and Muslims . . . in short, if everyone is an equal, then why is the second son not treated as an equal to the first? If a 'Committee for the Protection of the Second Son' had been formed, then I would have been saved the task of penning this boring biography. But in this country there is no place for those who mean well. You may find Animal Protection Committees—a dime a dozen—while second sons are just abandoned to fend for themselves. Look at any of the *avataars*. Each one of them is a first son. Just tell me if you know of any avataar who has an older brother dictating his every action? Younger brothers like Lakshman and Bharat have been crushed under the weight of a colossus like Ram. All younger brothers are cast only in a supporting role. See for yourself—Iffan was the elder son and so he was not bothered about his torn kurta. But Topi was so scared seeing his torn kurta that he completely forgot about the blood dripping from his face, knees, and elbow.

He started to cry.

'Are you very badly hurt?'

'No,' said Topi. 'You . . . not . . . see—my kurta torn?'

'Come, I'll wear you another kurta.'

'What kind of language you speaking?'

'This is how I always speak.'

Topi, of course, knew that this was how he spoke, but what he wanted to know was why he spoke the way he did. He spoke the way his Daadi did. He thought that this boy too belonged to his Daadi's party.

'You know my Daadi?' he asked.

'No,' said Iffan. 'I don't know your Daadi.'

'Then why are you speaking like her?'

Iffan started laughing. 'Perhaps your Daadi too is from Lucknow?'

'That I don't know,' he said and the matter ended there too. But he wasn't too happy. What if all the people of Lucknow belonged to Daadi's party?

'Come, come over to my house,' said Iffan, 'I'll show you my cycle. By the way, what is your name?'

'This Lucknow—where it is?'

'Very far from here.'

He drew some courage from this information—even if the whole of

Lucknow belonged to Daadi's party he need not worry as Lucknow was very far from here.

'My name—Balbhadra Narayan.'

'My name is Iff.'

'Such small name?'

'No. This is what I'm called at home.' This saddened Topi. He felt miserable for he did not even have a 'home-name'. 'Home names' are given only to those people who get called out to often at home. Nobody ever called out to Topi at home!

'You have cycle?' he asked.

'Yes. It came just yesterday.'

'Is it shining shining?'

'Yes.'

When he reached Iffan's house, he was engulfed by silence. He found this house rather strange. Strange kinds of crooked glasses, strange utensils, strange kinds of clothes—in short, the whole ambience was weird.

'Who is this?' asked an old woman.

'He is something Narayan.'

' Balbhadra,' said Topi.

'Whose son are you?' asked a young lady who turned out to be Iffan's mother.

'I am son of Dr Bhrugu Narayan.'

'That Blue Oil Doctor Bhrugu Narayan?' This was asked by a pleasant-faced man who turned out to be Iffan's father.

'Yes.'

'Iffan *miyaan*, get him something to eat,' said that man.

'You are MIYAAN?'

'Miyaan?' Iffan was stunned.

'You are Muslim?'

'Yes.'

'And these people?'

'This is my *Abbu*. This, my *Ammi* and this is my *Daada*.'

'I not asked that,' said Topi. 'Are these people also Muslim?'

'Yes.' Iffan's father smiled. 'We are miyaans.'

'Then I can't eat anything here.'

'Why?' This was Iffan's question.

'We people not eat food touched by miyaans.'

'But why?'

'Miyaans are very bad people.'

Everyone tried to coax him into eating something but he did not budge an inch. But when he saw Iffan's cycle he was overjoyed.

'From where you buy this?'

'My *chachu* has sent this from abroad.'

'Where is abroad?'

Iffan did not know the answer to this question. But he did not wish to admit that he did not know the answer. He pretended not to have heard this question and started cycling. And when the polished spikes of the cycle started sparkling, Topi himself forgot his question and started running after the cycle.

God knows for how long these two continued to play like this. But a servant came and put an end to this game.

'Little master, come, it is time for lunch.'

'Come, you too have lunch with me,' Iffan told Topi.

'No. I can't eat here.'

'Then miyaan, you too find your way home. People must be waiting for you for lunch there,' said the servant.

'I am not a miyaan.'

The servant left with Iffan. Topi stood alone in that big compound which was covered with a variety of fruit trees. Standing under one of those trees, he wondered why he did not have a cycle of his own. Amazingly, even Munni bhaiyya did not have a cycle! He smiled at the thought when he would proudly tell Munni bhaiyya that he had a friend who had a cycle bought for him by his chachu who lived abroad. Munni bhaiyya would be so disheartened! But—what is this chachu? Uh—must be something. What is important is that my friend has a cycle. This is how, one day, Topi quietly accepted Iffan as his friend. And in this newfound enthusiasm he even forgot that he had run away from home. He felt hungry. He walked towards home. But when he reached home he found that a strange silence had spread itself around his house. Ramdulari was expecting her third child.

'What would you like to have—a brother or a sister?' asked one of the servants.

'Can't I have a cycle?' asked Topi.

The old servant rollicked on the floor, holding her stomach, unable to contain her laughter. When she repeated what Topi wanted to have to two other young maids, they too started laughing, leaving Topi quite bewildered.

Later, this was passed on to his Daadi, Subhadradevi and his mother, Ramdulari as well. Ramdulari smiled. Subhadradevi lamented, in chaste Urdu, over Topi's idiocy. But not one of them thought about Topi's desire for a cycle. And when no one thought about this, he was automatically drawn towards Iffan.

If I have your permission, I'd like to tell you about Iffan at this juncture. It is against the very principles of a story or an autobiography to keep the reader in the dark. There is a difference between a reader and a consumer. There is a difference between a writer and a shopkeeper. The shopkeeper is interested in selling his wares—and so, like those who write thrillers, he shows a few things and hides a few others. But a novelist has nothing to sell. If the story is well constructed, then where is the need to lie to the reader? I want to tell you Topi's story without making it into a thriller because Topi's saga is the veritable theme of this era. This is a disgraceful era. Low people are being born. Beauty is covered with multi-coloured muck. This is not the era of great warriors and there is no time for the celebration of beauty either. No *yug* is a *Kaliyug*, but the Topi yug has most certainly commenced! That is why it is the duty of the novelist to introduce this yug to his reader and tell him where he stands in this rat race.

Krishna had told Arjun: 'I am Everything.' I am not Krishna—but I wish to tell the readers that I am Topi and I am Iffan too. I am Munni Babu and I am Bhairav! I am this yug and I am introducing myself to you. I am the writer and the reader. And the 'I' which is a writer, is seeking the permission of the 'I' that is the reader, to introduce Iffan.

It is important to know about Iffan because he is Topi's first friend. Topi has always called Iffan, Ifan, which Iffan has disliked. But he has always responded to the name Ifan. This was where his magnanimity lay—that he continued to respond. This whole issue about names too is a strange thing. Urdu and Hindi are the same language, just two names of Hindvi. But just see for yourself what happens when there are two different names. See how different names can cause trouble. If the name is Krishna—then it is an avataar. If the name is Mohammed—then it is a prophet. Caught in this quagmire of names, people have forgotten that both these men looked after milk-giving animals. Both were shepherds, both prayed to the formless, and both were nurtured by Braj.

This is why I say that Topi without Iffan or Iffan without Topi is not only incomplete but also a betrayal. That is why it is necessary to go to Iffan's house. It is important to know what kind of breeze blows in the garden of his soul and what kinds of fruits are being borne in the tree of tradition.

IV

Iffan's story, too, is very long. But we are concerned with Topi's story. So I won't tell you Iffan's complete story but only as much as is relevant to Topi's story.

No story can belong completely to one person. Whenever the novelist forgets this, then to make the hero look taller he starts cutting the other characters from the top or the bottom so that the hero is visible even from a distance. But stories are about other things too. Stories can never be about one person alone. Stories belong to all and yet its oneness remains intact.

The hero of this story is definitely Topi. But this story, or this biography, is not Topi's alone. This story is a slice of the story of this country, well . . . of this universe. A piece of *roti*, though separated from the main roti, retains all its qualities. That is why a novelist has to be cautious. He cannot kill or burn away characters at will. Premchand could not get Amarkaant and Sakeena married because that story is a slice of Indian life. Though pulled out from it, it is still a part of it. During Premchand's times, it was not possible for Amarkaant and Sakeena or Vijayalakshmi and Sayyed Hasan to get married.

That is why I thought it necessary to tell you a few things about Iffan because you are likely to see bits and pieces of him in several parts of this story. Neither is Topi a shadow of Iffan, nor is Iffan Topi's. These are two independent individuals who grew and developed independent of each other. These two inherited two different kinds of family traditions. These two had different thoughts about life. Yet, Iffan is an inseparable part of Topi's story. I am not talking here about Hindus and Muslims being like brothers. Why should I commit myself to this stupidity? Do I, each day, tell my younger or older brother that we are brothers? Even if I don't say such things, do you make such statements? If Hindus and Muslims are brothers then there is no need to be going around talking about it. And if they aren't, merely calling them brothers will not make a difference. I don't have to fight any elections. I am a storyteller and I am telling a story. I am talking about Topi and Iffan. These are two characters of this story. One is called Balbhadra Narayan Shukla and the other is Sayyed Zargaam Murtaza. One has been named Topi and the other, Iffan.

Iffan's Daada and great grandfather were very famous maulvis. Born in the land of the heathens. Died in the land of the heathens. But wrote in their wills that their bodies be taken to Karbala. Their souls did not take in a single breath in this land. The first Indian child to be born in this family grew up to be Iffan's father.

Iffan's father, Sayyed Murtaza Hussain, too, never ate anything touched by a Hindu. But when he died, he did not leave behind a will stating that his body be taken to Karbala. He was buried in an Indian grave.

Iffan's great grandmother too never ate anything touched by a Hindu. She was a very devout woman. Karbala, Nafaz, Khurasaan, Kaazmein—and God knows which other places she had travelled to. But whenever anyone had to leave home she would, without fail, keep a pot of water at the door and make propitiatry offerings of *dal* to the poor.

Iffan's grandmother, too, was quite particular about saying her *namaaz*, but when her only son was afflicted with chicken pox, she stood on one foot near the cot and said, '*Maata*, please forgive my child.' She belonged to the East. Was around nine or ten when she was married and had moved to Lucknow, but till her dying day she spoke her eastern dialect. The Urdu of Lucknow was what her in-laws spoke. She continued to embrace the language of her parents because, apart from this language, there was no one who could understand her heart's thoughts. When it was the day of her son's wedding, she was very keen to have song and dance celebrations. But how can you have singing and dancing in a maulvi's house? Poor thing, she just carried on, crushing her desires. But yes, during the ceremony performed on the sixth day of Iffan's birth and on the day of his circumcision she had the celebration of her choice and to her heart's content.

This was possible because Iffan was born after his Daada's death.

It is important to keep in mind this disparity between men and women, because without keeping this in mind you may not be able to understand the dynamics of Iffan's soul.

Iffan's grandmother was not a maulvi's but a zamindar's daughter. She had come to this house from her very well-to-do house. In her home, she used to be fed milk and butter. But after coming to Lucknow she used to yearn for the cream-soaked butter that her tenants would bring to her house in burnt vessels. Whenever she went to her mother's house, she would eat like a glutton. As soon as she returned to Lucknow, she would again have to become a *maulvin*. Her only complaint against her husband was this—that being uncaring for either time or opportunity, he always remained a maulvi.

She used to be perpetually restless in her in-laws' home. When she was dying, her son asked whether her body should be sent to Karbala or Nafaz. She got furious and said: '*Ay beta*, if you cannot take care of my dead body then send it to my own home.'

Because she was so close to dying she could not now remember where her house was. Her family had moved to Karachi and the house now belonged to a custodian. How can one remember these minor details on one's deathbed? This is the time when people see some of their most beautiful dreams. (This is what the author assumes, because he is not yet dead!) Iffan's Daadi too dreamt of her home. That house was called Kachchi Haveli. *Kachchi* because it was made of mud. She dreamt also about the Dasheri mango tree she had planted with her own hands and which, too, had grown old like her. She recalled several other small and beautiful things. How could she leave all these things and go to Karbala or Nafaz?

She was buried in Phaatmein in Benares because that is where Murtaza Hussain was posted during those days. Iffan was in school at that time. The servant came in with the news that Bibi had passed away. Iffan's Daadi used to be called Bibi.

At that time, Iffan was in the fourth standard and he had already met Topi.

Iffan loved his Daadi a great deal. In a sense, he also loved his Abbu, his Ammi, his *Baaji*, and little sister Nuzhat. But he loved his Daadi a little more than all the others. Ammi would occasionally scold or beat him. Baaji too was like that. Abbu too would sometimes mistake the house for a court and pass judgements. Whenever she got the opportunity, Nuzhat would draw pictures on his books. There was only Daadi who never hurt him in any way. At night she would tell him stories of Behram Daaku, Anaar Pani, Barah Burj, Ameer Hamza, Gulab Kaawli, Hatimtai, Panchfulla Rani, and others.

'When the world sleeps the Pure Creator remains awake. I am not telling you about something I've seen. I'm telling you something I've heard. There lived an emperor in a place. . . .'

He never laughed at Daadi's language. On the contrary, he quite liked it. But his Abbu never let him speak like that. And when he complained about this to his Daadi, she would laugh: 'Arre beta, why should you speak like an illiterate woman? You speak the way your father speaks.' That would be the end of the matter and a story would begin.

'So what did the emperor do—he promptly killed a deer. . . .'
This was the dialect that Topi found endearing. He saw Iffan's Daadi as belonging to his mother's party. He hated his grandmother. Hated her. God knows what kind of language she spoke. Iffan's father and his grandmother spoke the same language.

Whenever he went to Iffan's house he would try, as far as possible, to spend time with his Daadi. He would try, as far as possible, never to speak with Iffan's Ammi or Baaji. But these two women would keep prodding him to speak so that they could laugh at his dialect. But whenever the matter went out of hand, Daadi would intervene and bail him out: 'Why do you go there—near all those people—to get yourself teased like this? Come, you come here . . .' she would scold him. But each word would be like little toys of sugar. Like *amaavat*. Like *tilva*. And he would quietly go with her.

'So, what's your Ammi doing. . . .' This is how Daadi usually began her conversation. Earlier, he used to wonder what 'ammi' meant. Then he understood that they called 'maataji' Ammi.

He liked this word—Ammi. He chewed on this word like as if it were a piece of jaggery. Ammi. Abbu. Baaji.

Then a strange thing happened one day.

The twentieth century entered the house of Doctor Bhrugu Narayan Shukla of the Blue Oil, as well. Meaning, food began to be served on the table and there were chairs. What was kept on the table was the usual plate but no one sat on the floor any more.

What happened that day was that he liked the *baingan bharta* a little too much. Ramdulari was serving food.

Topi said: ' Ammi, some more baingan bharta.'

Ammi!

All the hands that were on the table froze. All eyes in the room fixed themselves on Topi's face.

Ammi! How did this corrupt word ammi, get into the house! The walls of tradition started shaking! Ammi! This was sacrilege, a religious crisis indeed.

'Where did you pick this *lubz* (word) from?' Subhadradevi asked.

'Lubz?' Topi's eyes twinkled. 'What's lubz, ma?'

'Who taught you to say ammi?' thundered his grandmother.

'I learnt this from Iffan.'

'What's his full name?'

'That I don't know.'

'Oh dear, who this is, this son of a miyaan, who you become friends with?' Ramdulari was shattered.

'*Bahu*, how many times do I have to tell you not to speak in that illiterate's dialect in my presence?' Subhadradevi fell like a ton of bricks on Ramdulari.

The context of the war changed.

These were also the days of the other war. That's why when Dr Bhrugu Narayan of Blue Oil came to know that Topi had befriended the Collector Saheb's son, he swallowed his anger and on the third day got the permit for clothes and sugar.

But that day was an unfortunate one for Topi. Subhadradevi got up from the table that very moment and Ramdulari once again started beating Topi.

'You will go again to that house?'

'Yes.'

'Oh dear, may your yes go underground and mingle with the dust.'

Ramdulari got tired of beating him. But Topi never once said that he would not go to Iffan's house. Munni Babu and Bhairav enjoyed watching Topi being beaten.

'One day I saw him at Rahim Meatman's shop eating meat,' Munni Babu added his bit.

Meat!

'Ram Ram Ram!' Ramdulari fell back two steps in disgust. Topi looked at Munni. The truth was that Topi had seen Munni Babu eating meat and Munni Babu had bribed him with a one-paisa coin. Topi also knew that Munni Babu smoked cigarettes. But he was not the sort to spill secrets. Till today, he had not mentioned anything about Munni Babu to anyone, except Iffan.

'You saw *me* eating meat?'

'Didn't I see you that day?' said Munni Babu.

'Then why didn't you say this that day itself?' asked Subhadradevi.

'He's a liar, Daadi!' said Topi.

Topi was deeply saddened that day. He was not grown up enough to understand the workings of truth and falsehood—and the truth is that he never really 'grew up' in that sense. That day he was so badly beaten up that his whole body ached.

One thought ran constantly in his mind—if only he could be older than Munni Babu for a day, for just a day, he would be able to understand things better. But it was not possible for him to be older than Munni Babu. He was born younger than Munni Babu and that's how things would remain.

The next day when he met Iffan in school, he told him all that had happened. Both missed their geography class. Iffan bought bananas from

Pancham's shop. The thing is that apart from fruit, Topi never touched other eatables offered by Iffan.

'Is it not possible for us to exchange our Daadis?' asked Topi. 'Your Daadi can come to my house and mine can be in yours. My Daadi too speaks just like you people.'

'That's not possible,' said Iffan. 'Abbu won't agree to this. And then who will tell me stories? Does your Daadi know the story of the Barah Burj?'

'You can't give me even one Daadi?' Topi could hear the sound of his heart breaking.

'She is my Daadi, but she is also my father's mother,' said Iffan.

Now Topi saw things more clearly.

'Your Daadi too must be old like mine?'

'Yes.'

'Then don't worry,' said Iffan. 'My Daadi says that old people die and go away.'

'My Daadi won't die.'

'How can she not die? You think my Daadi would lie?'

Exactly at this moment a servant came to inform that Iffan's Daadi had passed away.

Iffan left. Topi was left alone. Deeply disturbed, he went to the gymnasium. The old *chapraasi* was sitting to one side, smoking a *beedi*. Topi went to a corner and started weeping.

When he went to Iffan's house in the evening, everything was deathly still. The house was crowded. There were more than the usual number of people at home. But without Daadi the house seemed empty to Topi—strange thing, considering that he did not even know Daadi's name. In spite of her pleading with him a thousand times he never ate a single morsel of what she offered him. Love is not determined by these things. There was a bond between Topi and Daadi—a kind of bond that went beyond the Muslim League, the Congress, and the Janasangh.

Had Iffan's Daada been alive, he too, like Topi's family members, would not have been able to comprehend this kind of a friendship. They were two separate halves, incomplete selves. One completed the other. Both were thirsty. One quenched the other's thirst. Both were strangers in their own home and were alone in a crowded house. Both wiped out the other's loneliness. One was seventy-two years old and the other was eight.

'If my Daadi had died instead of yours things would have been so much better,' Topi consoled Iffan.

Iffan did not reply. He did not know what to say to this. The two friends started weeping silently.

V

On the 10th of October 1945, Topi took a vow never to make friends with any boy whose father had a transferable job.

The date 10 October 1945 has in itself no significance, but in the history of Topi's spiritual growth this date is important, for it was on this date that Iffan's father left for Muradabad on a transfer. This change took place just a few days after Iffan's Daadi's death and left Topi even more alone because not one of the three sons of the next collector, Thakur Harinamsingh, could become Topi's friend. Dabbu was too young. Beelu, too old. Guddu was the same age as Topi but he spoke only in English. And these three were far too conscious of the fact that they were the Collector's sons. No one was interested in Topi.

The gardener and chapraasi knew Topi. And so he could enter the bungalow. Beelu, Guddu, and Dabbu were playing cricket at that time. Dabbu hit the ball. The ball came straight at Topi's face. Out of sheer fear Topi raised his hands to cover his face. The ball fell right into his hands.

'How's that?'

The head gardener was the umpire. He raised his finger. The poor fellow only knew that whenever anyone shouted 'Hows that' he had to raise his finger.

'Who are you?' asked Dabbu in English.

'Balbhadra Narayan,' said Topi.

'Who is your father?' This was Guddu.

'Bhrugu Narayan.'

'Ay.' Beelu called out to the umpire.

'Who is Bhrugu Narayan? Is he any one of our chapraasis?'

'No, Saheb,' said the umpire. 'He is a famous daagdar of this city.'

'You mean doctor?' asked Dabbu.

'Yes sir!' The head gardener had picked up this bit of English.

'But he looks so clumsy,' said Beelu.

'Ay,' called out a furious Topi. 'Just mind your tongue. One tight slap and you'll start dancing.'

'Oh you son of a dirty pig,' and Beelu slapped Topi. Topi fell to the ground and got up swearing expletives. The head gardener intervened and Dabbu called out to his Alsatian.

Topi came back to his senses only when seven needles had been pricked into his stomach. And after that he never saw the collector's bungalow again. Then there was this question about what exactly it was that he ought to do. All said and done there was only Sita, the old maid at home, who could understand his hurt and pain. So he went straight under her wings. And once he took refuge there, his soul too became small. Everyone in the house, whether young or old, would scold her. Everyone in the house, young or old, scolded Topi too. And so the two grew fond of each other.

'Don't instigate them babu.' One night when Munni Babu and Bhairav beat him up for picking up a quarrel with them, she took him to her room and tried to explain things to him.

What had happened was that it was wintertime. There was a new coat meant for Munni Babu. Bhairav too got a new coat. Topi was given Munni Babu's coat. The coat was new but because Munni Babu had not liked it, it was given away to Topi. But still, it had been made for Munni Babu, right? It was a hand-me-down, a leftover. That very moment Topi handed the coat over to the other maid, Ketaki's son. That boy was happy. Now you cannot take back what you have given to the servants, can you? So it was decided that Topi should forego the coat and just as well have a taste of the winter cold.

'I don't want the cold, I'd much rather have food,' said Topi.

'You can have a taste of my slippers,' said Subhadradevi.

'Don't you even know this that slippers cannot be tasted, they can only be worn?'

'You are being rude to Daadi,' said an angry Munni Babu.

'Then what do you expect me to do—worship her?'

Well . . . what do you think could have happened? Daadi created a scene, shouted, screamed. Ramdulari started beating Topi again.

'You are in the tenth standard child,' said Sita. 'You should not speak in this manner to her. Because, all said and done, she is your Daadi.'

It was very easy for Sita to say glibly that he was in the tenth standard.

But this was no easy achievement at all. He had had to struggle a great deal to move up to the tenth standard. He had even failed for two years. He had moved to the ninth standard way back in 1949. But he could reach the tenth standard only in 1952.

When he failed for the first time, Munni Babu had stood first in his Intermediate and Bhairav in his sixth. Everyone in the house took him to task. He wept a lot. It was not as if he was a duffer. On the contrary, he was quite smart. But no one ever allowed him to study. Whenever he would sit down to study, Munni Babu would have some work for him, or else Ramdulari would want him to buy things for which she could have sent her servants—and if it weren't one of these, he would learn that Bhairav had used his notes to make aeroplanes and fly them.

The next year he had typhoid. The third year he passed in the third division. This 'third division' clung on to him throughout his life.

But we have to also take into account his problems. In 1949, he was with his friends. He failed. His friends moved on ahead. He remained behind. In 1950, he had to sit in the same class with those boys who had been in the eighth standard the previous year.

It is not an easy thing to sit with students who are junior to you. His friends were in the tenth. He would continue to meet them, play with them. He could not become friends with those who were in his present class. Every time he sat in class, he felt strange. And to add to this discomfort, whenever his teacher wanted to pull up a weaker student, he would use Topi as an example.

'What is this, Shyam Avataar (or Muhammed Ali)? You too want to stay on in this class like Balbhadra?'

The whole class would burst into laughter at such remarks. Those who laughed were the ones who had been in the eighth standard the previous year.

Somehow or the other he managed to put up with this class. But when in 1951 too he had to sit in the same class he became like pulp, because now he would have no friends even in the tenth standard. The eighth standard students were now in the tenth. He was with the seventh standard students! He seemed quite an old fellow in their midst.

As in his crowded home, so also in school—he became alone. The teachers more or less stopped noticing his presence. Whenever a question was asked and he too would raise his hand to answer, the teacher would never give him a chance to speak. But once when he raised his hand for every question that was asked, his English Literature teacher taunted him with: 'You have been learning the same text for the last three years, no wonder you have the answers to all the questions! These boys have to appear for the High School Exam next year. I'll ask you the year after that.'

Topi was so embarrassed that even his dark face reddened. And when the other students started laughing, he almost died. When he had come to the ninth for the first time, he too was a child just like them.

That same day, during recess, Abdul Waheed shot an arrow that went straight to Topi's heart.

Waheed was the most intelligent boy in class. Was also the monitor. And most important, he was the son of Doctor Sharfuddin of the Red Oil.

He said, 'Balbhaddar! How dare you try to be a part of us? You should make friends with the eighth standard students. We will move on, you will have to stay on with them.'

This comment killed Topi and he took a vow, no matter what, typhoid or whatever, he had to pass his exams.

But there were elections in between.

Doctor Bhrugu Narayan of the Blue Oil stood for these elections. Now if someone in your house stands for the elections can anyone study in that house?

It was only when the Doctor Saheb lost his deposit that there was some quiet in the house and Topi realized that his exams were just round the corner.

He started studying. But how can anyone study in such an environment? That is why his passing the exams itself has to be seen as a major achievement.

'Wah!' said Daadi. 'God protect him from evil eyes. Quite a good pace. Passed in the third grade in the third attempt at least!'

'While Sharfua's son has passed in the first grade,' said Doctor Saheb. (He used to call Dr Sharfuddin as Sharfua.)

Topi hated Abdul Waheed. It wasn't his fault that he had passed in the first grade. And he was also in no way responsible for Topi passing in the third grade. But the way in which he was being compared to Waheed was very bitter indeed to have to swallow.

He also met a few new people during that time. These people would bring all the boys from the neighbourhood together and teach them wrestling, teach them to march, to do tricks with batons, and generally talk to them.

All of a sudden, Topi found himself getting closer to these people. They took him into their fold with open arms. Then when he learnt that these people belonged to the party that had killed Gandhiji, he got scared. But he continued to meet them.

It was from these people that he learnt, for the first time, about the ways in which Muslims had ruined this country. All the mosques in the country had been built by demolishing temples that stood in that place. (Topi was suspicious about this information because two mosques in the city had come up in his presence and there was no demolition of any temple 'wemple'.) Killing cows was one of the favourite pastimes of the Muslims. Then they were responsible for the partition of the country. They had brutally murdered lakhs of old people and children in Punjab and Bengal. They had raped women and there were few atrocities that these Muslims had not committed. As long as these Muslims remained here, this country could not prosper. And so it was the duty of every Hindu youth to push the Muslims into the Arabian Sea.

All these statements did have their impact. Sometimes, in the midst of all this talk, he would think of Iffan. But when Waheed stood first he was convinced that as long as the Muslims remained in this country, a Hindu could not be at peace.

So, like a true Indian and a true Hindu, he began hating the Muslims.

And when in the July of 1952 he went to school, he became a Janasanghi. That's why when Sita taunted him with the remark that he was in the tenth, he got furious. He said: 'Daadi speaks the language of the miyaans. I think that she has become a Muslim.'

VI

Iffan's life, on the other hand, had taken an entirely different route. He was not interested in politics but he could not escape the politically loaded conversations that took place at home. And even if his interest lay only in the 'Sports' page, he had to hold the entire newspaper in his hands.

The things that he heard and the things that he read in the newspapers were enough to make his hair stand on end. He was fascinated by literature. Wamik Jhaunpuri, Sahir Ludhianvi, Ali Sardar Jaffrey, and the poems of other poets and Krishan Chandar Abbas and the novels of other novelists told him that something had gone wrong somewhere with this freedom.

> Who has become free?
> From whose forehead has the blot of slavery been wiped out?
> This Punj-ab now is no more a pleasant dream.
> It is but a Do-ab, this Punjabni is now fire.
> Allah stood still in the Jama Masjid.
> And darkness lingered in Chandni Chowk.
> Like an unbaked earthen pot hope floated away
> Sohni kept wobbling mid-stream.
> I ask Warris Shah
> Speak, speak from under some tomb
> And today from the Book of Love
> Let's turn open a new page.

And today from the Book of Love let's turn open a new page! Pages from the Book of Love were lying scattered in the storm, were rotting like corpses, and echoing all around like screams. They were counting the dead bodies that arrived by the Peshawar Express. Like a prostitute's letter, they were searching for Nehru and Mohammed Ali Jinnah. . . .

'The Sikhs have done such strange things. They have paled little children on the blades of their *kirpaan*. Thirty Sikhs together have violated a thirteen-year-old girl. The poor girl died sometime during the act. . . .'

He could hear snatches of this conversation coming from Abbu's room while he was sitting in the courtyard reading the story *Sardarji* written by Khwaja Ahmed Abbas.

That was a *Mistake*. The echo of another story by Manto floated in.

But who had committed the mistake? No one answered this question.

The tender conscience of a fourteen or fifteen year old was groping in the jungle of these questions. Fire raged in the garden of life from Dhaka to Peshawar. The harvested crops were burning. The crops yet to be harvested were burning. Thick acrid smoke hovered between the ground and the skies. There was hardly any space to breathe.

'Abbu, are these Hindus very bad people?' he asked his father one day. 'And these Sikhs? They seem to be absolute savages.'

At that time he did not know that Hindus and Sikhs belonging to East and West Pakistan could be asking their fathers similar questions about Muslims.

His question was a simple one but his father could not give him a simple answer. The newspapers reported something but his conscience said something else—and the smoke that was trapped around choked him.

Yet, he had to give an answer.

'No, son,' said Abbu. 'Bad people are not Hindus or Muslims.'

'But . . .'

'I too am aware of what's happening,' said Abbu in a sharp tone, cutting off his remarks. Iffan was perplexed. His father always used to smile. What was happening? What exactly was it that was happening?

'Where's the need to scold him?' said Ammi. 'Yes, son, these Hindus and Sikhs are very bad people.'

'Why?' asked Iffan. Ammi was taken aback. 'And why exactly has Allah miyaan created such bad people?'

'The fruits of their sin, son,' said Ammi.

'What sins could those children have committed?'

'That's enough now, just shut up.' Ammi too was annoyed.

That day, for the first time, his regard for Allah miyaan declined. It seemed hardly fair that the children should pay for the sins of their elders.

This mistrust was a dangerous thing. It immediately disarmed him. Allah miyaan was no different from the Hindus and the Sikhs.

That night he dreamt that Allah miyaan's white beard was smeared with red blood and He was making a speech addressing a congregation of Hindus and Sikhs.

'How has this Muslim child come here?' Allah miyaan pointed towards him. 'Kill him!'

As soon as the congregation heard this, they pounced on him. An old Sardarji happened to be coming from the other side. Iffan thought that now he was truly done for. But this Sardarji quickly hid him inside his turban. The congregation of people surrounded him. One of them lashed out a sword and in a jiffy the Sardarji's head was severed from his body. His head rolled to the ground and started running. The crowd started chasing that head. The head entered into an assembly where a semi-clad old man, wearing an old pair of glasses, was seated and was saying something. The head slid behind that man. A gunshot was heard. The old man with the pair of glasses fell dead.

The Sardarji's head started running again.

A book shop was burning. Jawaharlal Nehru looked strange in the glow of the flames of his books. That head said: 'I am Ahmed Abbas' *Sardarji*. Here, take this. Take care of your property. . . .'

His turban uncoiled. Iffan leapt out and slipped into the pocket of Panditji's *jawahar* jacket.

'Who are you?' asked Jawaharlal.

'I am Iffan.'

'No,' said Jawaharlal. 'You are India. I have got you back again today. I'll write a book on you again.'

The crowd reappeared. All the Hindus and Sikhs were wearing Jinnah caps. Quite a few were wearing Turkish caps. A date palm tree was peeping out of the collars of a few people's *sherwanis*.

Jawaharlal looked at the crowd. His face flushed with rage. Taking Iffan with him he jumped into the fire where the books were burning. Iffan screamed.

His eyes opened.

Children who grow up under the shade of falling walls have bizarre stories to tell.

When Iffan opened his eyes, his soul crept into its shell.

He got up as he did every day. As usual, he washed his hands and face and greeted his parents. He received blessings from them just as he did everyday. He went to school as usual. But the people in school appeared strange and different. He felt that Babu Triveni Narayan slapped him hard but did not slap Lakshman just as hard, while both of them had been guilty of the same offence. He felt that the Chowdhariji explained an answer to Ramdas with greater attention but explained things to him in a perfunctory manner. . . .

All his friends in school seemed to be like strangers. He found himself absolutely alone. He felt as if his sherwani were a little too heavy for his shoulders. That day he quietly vowed to himself that he would wear the sherwani all his life.

During the games period the students were playing football. Iffan was good at this game. The defendent from the other team kicked him. Iffan slipped and fell. There was nothing unusual about this. But today he was furious. He took his revenge immediately. The other boy too fell. Master Saheb shouted at Iffan and asked him to leave the field. The boys continued to play while Iffan stood alone outside the field. He thought that if he weren't a Muslim, Master Saheb would not have turned him out like this.

That evening when he reached home his mother saw that he looked upset and sad. His mother kissed him. She gave him the halwa that Mamuji had got from Delhi. He ate it without relishing it. She could not bring the colour back to his cheeks.

'What's the matter with you miyaan?' asked the Delhi Mamu.

'Nothing.'

'Looks like you were beaten up in school,' said Mamu, laughing.

'Pakistan has been made by the Muslims, isn't it?' he asked.

'No.' said Mamu. 'Pakistan has been made by the British.'

'You are the only one who says this,' he said. 'What I want to say is that if Muslims have made Pakistan then what are we doing here? Abbu, why don't we go to Pakistan?'

'Why are you ruining your time thinking about these things?' said Abbu.

'Because the Hindu master does not explain things well to me,' he said. 'Hindu boys trouble me. The day before, my hands touched Bhavani's sweet box by mistake and he threw away the sweets and said 'Arre miyaan, this is not Pakistan.'

'Ok. Now you tell me this. When you went to *Nana* Saheb's house, didn't Gaurishankar Saheb treat you well?' asked Mamu.

'He did.'

'And isn't he a Hindu?'

'But Mamujaan, why are such Hindus not here?'

'Miyaan, your Nana does not eat anything touched by the Hindus, but doesn't he continue to be friends with Gaurishankar?'

'That's true, but . . .'

'In the same way, if your friend Bhavani does not eat food touched by you, why should you feel affronted?'

'Because he mentioned that Pakistan bit to me.'

'If someone tells you that the crow has run away with your ears—what will you do—see if your ears are in place or run after the crow? Did you make Pakistan?'

'Not at all.'

'Then why do you get angry?'

Iffan got the hang of things, but a nameless fear still persisted. He continued to go to school, but gradually drifted away from his Hindu friends. Shankar, Ramdeen, Prabhu, Bhavani, Seetaram . . . he couldn't build any meaningful rapport with any of them. Now all around him were Wajid, Muhibbul Hasan, Sarvar—other kinds of names. From among his older group of friends only Mujavir and Jamaal remained.

No one noticed this change. The master continued to teach. The boys continued to study. The master did not think it important to find out the basis on which boys made friends these days.

The boys too did not spare a minute to think about why they had moved away from their older group of friends and why they had become friends with boys who hadn't previously been their friends.

The Maulvi who taught Urdu, however, realized that his class had shrunk—and that no Hindu boy now came to study Urdu.

One day he told his wife, 'If things continue like this, there will be no one to study Urdu.'

'Then why don't we go away to Pakistan?' his wife asked.

'I'll be retiring in two years,' said the Maulvi. 'I have lived here all my life, why should I go there to die!'

'Talking about life and death all the time,' muttered his wife angrily. 'Two daughters sitting at home like mountains. What are we to do—make pickles out of them?'

'You know I've written to my brother Kaleemullah. There are plenty of Muslim boys in Karachi.'

Now how can a Maulvi, bogged down by the burden of two unmarried daughters, do justice to the love poems of Ghalib?

Whenever he took the roll call, his heart would become heavy. Muhammed Haneef, Akarmullah, Badrul Hassan, Nazaf Abbas, Bakaullah, Muhammed Umar Siddiqui, Hizbr Ali Khan Tokhi. . . . He would get bored calling out the same kind of names. What happened to all those Aasharam, Narbada Prasad, Matadeen, Gaurishankar Sinha, Madholal Agarwal, Maseeh Peter, Raunak Lal. . . .

He was deeply hurt by the thought that the Hindi Pandit's register was brimming with names. The colourful diversity of names had left his register and had settled in Panditji's.

He was full of ire against the Panditji who had snatched away his treasure. So he started speaking ill of Hindi.

'Holy trouble! What kind of a tongue is this! Two words and the poor tongue starts panting for breath.'

When these words reached Panditji, he felt very bad. He spoke very good Urdu and Persian. But he had stopped speaking in Urdu to retaliate against the Maulvi Saheb. He had trouble speaking in Hindi. But now he spoke only in Hindi. He tried hard to forget those Urdu-Persian words that so naturally tripped off his tongue.

This strained atmosphere increased to such an extent that Maulvi Saheb did not recommend Panditji's name to the school's Annual Mushaaira Committee. The *mushaaira* took place. But the boys created a racket. And right on the heels of the mushaaira, Panditji organized a *kavi-sammelan*. This was the first time that the city had had a kavi-sammelan. Money came pouring in from Mahajan's party. The kavi-sammelan was a grand success. But later, Panditji confessed to one of his friends, Maulvi Ahamdullah Advocate: 'You know—no matter what, one can't reproduce the ambience of a mushaaira.'

Maulvi Ahamdullah, who was the President of the Zilla Congress Committee and had once been the President of the Zilla Muslim League, said: 'Panditji, traditions are not made in a day. Wait and see, in a short time, people would have forgotten mushaairas.'

Panditji didn't quite like this point of view, but kept quiet. And Maulvi Ahamdullah Saheb decided on his way home that he would have his younger son, Kurbaan Ali and daughter, Aayeshbano trained in Hindi as the future of Urdu seemed bleak.

That same night when Iffan recited to his Ammi a poem that had been hugely acclaimed in the kavi-sammelan, she smiled and said: 'Let the language go to the dogs. Is this any language at all? The toilet cleaners in my town speak a more beautiful language.'

'From now on we will have only this language,' said Abbu, who had attended the sammelan in his capacity as a Zilla head. If he had chosen not to attend the sammelan then the people of the city would have said that he did not come because he was a Muslim Collector.

' Why will we have only this language Abbu?'

'You'll understand when you grow up some more.'

'Will this language be popular because it belongs to the Hindus?'

'What nonsense is this—every minute you keep talking about Hindus and Muslims,' admonished his father.

He'd been noticing for some years now that his father was getting to be quite irritable for no apparent reason. But he was not able to understand why his father had become like that.

But that was how things were.

VII

The way I keep coming back every now and then to talking about Iffan—please do not even for a minute assume that this story is about both Topi and Iffan. Not at all. This is a story only about Topi. But it is important to keep flitting into Iffan's consciousness every now and then, because one cannot see the changes happening in the country merely from Topi's frame of vision. Iffan, too, is a varied form of Topi. This Topi has a myriad forms. In Bengal, Punjab, UP, Andhra, Assam . . . in the entire country, this Topi, burdened with his problems, is knocking at the doors of ideologies, philosophies, politics. . . . But no one supports him. I cannot expand the story to include all the forms of Topi. So I have chosen only two forms of Topi.

These two forms both clash with each other and, at the same time, are each incomplete without the other. The question that confronts Topi—or Topis—is one of legacy, of traditions, loves and hates, of trusts, doubts, and fears.

From Kabir to Golwalkar, and from Khusru to Sadar Ayyub. And whatever was before Khusru and Kabir. And all that which will happen after Golwalkar's and Ayyub's times. Topi is in the midst of this fatal whirlpool.

Topi is born, in every era, in the very lap of fatal whirlpools. In every era, he is born in the shade of falling walls and it takes him several days to clear off the debris from his body. And during these times, he is absolutely alone and without support. No one understands the language he speaks. But the Topi that we are pursuing is the most difficult one compared to the Topis of all previous eras. Today we cannot speak highly of him.

Every Topi today is a Janasanghi, a Congressman, a Communist, a member of the Muslim League, and all such things. Today, his statement to the world is a multitude of broken phrases. And each phrase speaks in a new language—and thinks in a different manner. That is why we have to keep going, again and again, towards Iffan.

When Iffan moved into the days of his youth, he grew without dreams. He continued to study. Moved from one grade to the other. But did not know what it was that he had to do. For years, no Muslim name had appeared in the IAS and IFS lists. Iffan did not pause to think that there were a lot of Hindu names too that did not make it to the list. He just did not take these exams. And when, despite keeping his eyes open through the night, no dream filtered in, he decided to let his beard grow. He still wasn't too happy with Allah miyaan's role. But he was a fellow-member of a scared generation and so he said the namaaz regularly.

After his father passed away, the burden of looking after his younger brothers and sisters fell upon him. Baaji had already relocated to Pakistan with her husband. She kept asking him to come there. But Iffan did not go to Pakistan. He was scared. He wanted to overcome this fear.

He found a job as a lecturer of History in one of the degree colleges. He was very happy. He prepared a great deal for the first class. But when he entered the classroom he saw boys with dimmed eyes sitting like corpses. No soul peeped from the windows of any eye. Their eyelids were drooping. It was as if the owner of the house, while fleeing from home in fear, had forgotten to shut the windows. And the windows kept opening and shutting in the breeze. Shutting and opening. The glass panes were cracking. The latches had become half-dead with the effort of resisting the rains.

Iffan saw the class and was shocked.

What could he teach these boys? How would these boys ever understand that when two rivers meet they become one—not three? How could he convince them that history was not the name given to different periods or different moments, but that history was the autobiography of time? The Panipat wars, the Buxor war, or the Battle of Plassey were just bubbles in this river. . . .

Muslim Rajput Degree College!

It wasn't as if only Muslim Rajputs studied here. Sheikh, Sayyed, Pathaans—they were all there. The college had Hindu, Rajput, Kayasth, Bhoomihar, Thakur, Aheer, and Kurmi boys—but in the History class there was only one Hindu student.

One day, the class happened to get into a discussion about Aurangazeb and Shivaji Maratha. Iffan was of the opinion that people like Prithviraj Chauhan and Shivaji were reactionaries because they interrupted the flow of the concept of Indian Nationalism.

That lone Hindu boy, Chandrabali Singh, stood up and rattled off the views of historians like Guru Golwalkar and K.M. Munshi.

'Sir! The Mughal emperors destroyed the ancient Indian culture. The era of Mughal rule is the blackest era in the history of Indian culture. Is there a single mosque that is half as beautiful as any of the ancient temples? It is because of this sense of inferiority that Aurangazeb had temples demolished. . . .'

Iffan was stunned beyond words. But he was a teacher of History. He had to say something in such a situation: 'When molten lead was being poured into the ears of the untouchables, were the high caste Hindus suffering from an inferiority complex . . . ?'

The entire lecture was consumed by this discussion. Chandrabali refused to see Iffan's point of view and Iffan did not agree with Chandrabali's point of view. But that evening Iffan returned home a very saddened man.

'What's the matter?' asked his wife, Sakeena.

He told her. 'And if these are the kinds of arguments being drilled into students' heads, what will happen to this country? The newer generation is at a greater loss than ours. We have no dreams. But this generation has false hopes. I teach History. It seems as if Hindustan is not destined to have a history at all. I was taught a history written by the British. Chandrabali is being taught a history written by the Hindus. The same thing must be happening in Pakistan. Their history may bear an Islamic stamp. Wonder when Hindustani history will ever be written.'

'I've been telling you . . . let's go away to Pakistan,' said Sakeena.

'To teach that before the Muslims came the Hindustanis were uncivilized?' He shook his head to mean a 'no'. 'No! Both nations are chasing a mirage. It's best that I quit teaching.'

There was another problem he faced while teaching. The boys understood neither English nor the language he spoke. While he taught, he watched how his voice banged against their flat faces and returned to him.

He still managed to pull through for a year. But that very year, the son of the Secretary of the Managing Committee completed his M.A. in history. There was a need to create a vacancy for him. So a story was planted in the newspapers of the city that Iffan belonged to the Muslim League. That he praises Aurangazeb and ridicules Shivaji.

The Managing Committee asked him for an explanation. During that time there was a vacancy in the Muslim University. Iffan was an 'old boy' of that University and was accepted.

And this is how in the year 1960, he met Topi again.

VIII

Topi and Aligarh Muslim University? It is possible that quite a few of you may find this piece of news surprising, because we had left Topi at a point where he was planning to become a part of the Janasangh. Then what had he come to Aligarh for—the very hub of Muslim communalism?

Had I been just a novelist and nothing else I would have ignored this question. But remember what I am telling you here is not a story but a biography. Topi came to Aligarh only to have an idea of the kinds of dreams the Muslim youth were dreaming.

You see, there used to be only three kinds of dreams earlier—those seen by children, by the youth, and by the old. And then a few things got added on to this list—like the dream for independence. And later still, a great churning took place in the world of dreams. Dreams of mothers and fathers started clashing with those of sons and daughters. The father wants the son to be a doctor and the son settles down as a full-timer in the Communist party. This is not the only kind of change happening. A million different dreams have sprouted like worms at monsoon time. Dreams of clerks. Dreams of labourers. Dreams of mill-owners. Dreams of becoming film stars. Hindi dreams. Urdu dreams. Hindustani dreams. Pakistani dreams. Hindu dreams. Muslim dreams. The whole nation is trapped in this quicksand of dreams. In this bustle of dreams, the dreams of children, of the youth, and of the old have been shred to bits. The dreams of Hindu children, of the Hindu old, and the Hindu youth are now separate from the dreams of Muslim children, Muslim old, and the Muslim youth. Dreams have become Bengali, Punjabi, and Uttar Pradeshi.

What the politicians saw was only this—that one day a piece of Hindustan moved away and got named Pakistan. If all that had happened was simply this then there would have been no need to be afraid of anything. But the dreams got into a messy tangle and the hands and feet of litterateurs were severed. Individuals, nations, and eras have the prerogative to dream. But these days, individuals in our country do not have dreams. The eyes of the nation are in pain because they have been awake for so long. As for the eras—they have forgotten what it means to have dreams.

Come to think of it, on what grounds can anyone dream?

But the crisis is that no one is aware of this crisis of dreams because each one, in his opinion, believes he has some dream or the other.

That is why Topi too has a dream. There was this issue of the scholarship. Topi had applied for it. But the scholarship was given to a Muslim candidate. And that Muslim boy was no great scholar or anything of that sort. He did not even have any relative among the people who handed over this scholarship. But one of his father's friends (who belonged to the Janasangh), was a member of the Committee. Politics has its place; and friendship, its place. This scholarship went to that boy. The thought that one Muslim boy got a scholarship after eliminating seven hundred and twenty-two Hindu boys angered Topi. So he started having dreams of winning a scholarship from the Aligarh Muslim University.

At the same time, his conscience was constantly troubled by the question of the need for a Muslim University considering that now Pakistan had already been created.

And the third reason was that he wanted to know what the Indian Muslim youth thought, what kinds of dreams they had.

But on coming to Aligarh, he got trapped with certain kinds of people and his whole programme was grounded. Sardar Jogendra Singh. Hamid Rizvi. Ikhtidaar Aalam. K.P. Singh.... A small group of Hindu, Muslim, and Sikh boys were waging a war within the University campus itself. These boys belonged to the S.F.

Munni Babu had cautioned him, while he was preparing to leave, that in Aligarh he had to fear not the Muslims so much as the Communists. But he could not save himself from this group of people.

How could he ask Ikhtidaar Aalam to shut up—he was just as passionately opposed to Pakistan as Topi was. How could he tell that Hamid Rizvi to stay away—he had been beaten up by some Muslim boys because he had demanded that kavi-sammelans should be held along with mushaairas and that instead of lectures merely on Islam, the Union should have lectures on all religions. Janmaasthami should be celebrated along with Milad-e-Nabi....

These were the very people who would nominate Hindu candidates for Union elections and canvas for their victories, get beaten up in the process, lose elections, but never lose heart.

'What are you afraid of?' Hamid asked one day. 'Aren't you from the majority community? What can four crore Muslims do to damage thirty crore Hindus?'

'They were less than four crores when they bloody demolished temples and built their mosques.'

'Why did the Hindus allow them to be demolished?' asked Jogendra.

'Listen Shukla,' said K.P., 'that's not the issue. If we try to settle accounts of the past, it will take us till tomorrow. We have four crore Muslims here with us now. And they will remain here.'

'Why should they remain here?'

'Because we belong here.' Ikhtidaar was getting furious. Whenever Ikhtidaar got angry he went red in the face. 'This is what is called Hindu chauvinism—why should they remain here? The way you ask this as if your father owns this country.'

'That's the truth,' said Topi. 'If it is not my father's then what do you think? That it belongs to your father? God knows how you have come uninvited and now claim to be family members.'

'And your ancestors grew directly from under this soil like the *sirfal* tree, is it?'

'Please Ikhtidaar,' said Jogendra.

'No miyaan,' said Ikhtidaar pushing his hand away. 'These Hindus think no end of themselves. Read history. History! Everybody has come from somewhere else here . . .'

The matter had clearly gone out of hand. Topi stood up but Ikhtidaar remained seated. And when Topi finished blowing hot and cold, he started laughing.

'Come on now, treat me to a cup of tea and order for two bottles of your father's Blue Oil for all the Congressmen. The tracks of their political paths have become rusted.'

'Arre, who is this bearded man who has joined you?' Hamid asked Jogendra.

'So, ultimately you remain a junior only, right?' Jogendra laughed. 'Arre Bhai. This is that same Zargaam Saheb. He used to belong to the times when there were nightingales. But by God, what a speaker he is! Sayeed Anda used to say that he is a better speaker than Sultan Niyazi and Munis Saheb.'

'Oh, come off this,' said K.P. 'How can you compare Sultan Niyazi and Munis Bhai with this bum?'

'He's been a topper in M.A.,' said Jogendra. 'And Dr Tarachand has praised his dissertation so highly that you might not believe it.'

'But this is an awfully third-rate behaviour yaar—that you top your M.A. course and wear a beard,' said Ikhtidaar.

'Where does this Jarghaam Saheb come from?' asked Topi.

'Not Jarghaam, Zargaam!' corrected K.P.

'Wah!' said Jo, Ikhtidaar, and Hamid simultaneously.

A fine had to be paid for not getting the sound nuances right and, finding fault with the Urdu language and Arabic words, K.P. took everyone with him to Café de Fuse.

The boys sitting at the adjacent table were talking about some girl. And on the other side, a senior *Mullah* was treating a circle of friends to tea and talking animatedly against the Communists.

'. . . this University is not scared of the Hindus. But is scared of the Communists. Dr Zakir Hussain speaks of an age-old rivalry. There is no department where these Communists have not sneaked in. Look at Allah's grace that the girls of a Muslim University are seen dancing and *Antony and Cleopatra* is being staged in the name of culture.'

'This is an absolutely wrong thing to do,' said K.P. 'Muslim girls should stage only *Laila-Majnu* and *Sheeri-Farhaad*.'

Boys from the other tables nearby started laughing. From among those who laughed, the Muslims laughed more than the Hindus.

'Why are you spoiling this Blue Oil recruit, partner?' asked the senior Mullah.

K.P. would definitely have had an answer to this but at that very moment Iffan arrived there with another lecturer.

'*Saalek*,' K.P. greeted him.

'Saalek,' replied Iffan. 'So, whose purse is being lightened today?'

'It's K.P.'s turn sir,' said Jo and added, 'welcome.'

The two lecturers sat down at that table.

'I've heard that your play was a great success,' said Iffan to K.P. 'I had to leave for Delhi that very day. Sorry I wasn't able to see the play. Who is this gentleman here?' He indicated towards Topi.

'Bhai, go ahead and speak out your name,' said Bhai Khan. 'His name has seeped a little into the national language, sir!'

Iffan smiled.

'Balbhadra Narayan Shukla.'

Iffan got a start.

'Where have you come from?'

'From Benares.'

'Arre, aren't you the son of Doctor Bhrugu Narayan?'

'Yes, I am.'

'So, your Daadi has sent you all the way here to learn Urdu?'

'Iffan!' Topi's eyes sparkled. 'Since when you having beard?' asked Topi breaking into dialect.

'This is my childhood friend,' Iffan told K.P. and the others. 'He was to have a brother and his servant asked him if he wanted a brother or a sister. Our man said—can't I have a cycle?'

There was such a burst of laughter that the roof of Café de Fuse literally shook and the sparrows nibbling sugar particles on a nearby table flew off in fear.

'Saheb, we never thought he was this strange!' said Ikhtidaar.

'That is why he has left Benares and come to Aligarh to do an M.A. in Hindi!' K.P. added his bit.

'So, have you started eating food touched by miyaans?' asked Iffan. 'And what's happened to that terrific tuft of hair on your head?'

'I've lent them to your beard,' said Topi, a trifle bitterly. Nobody laughed. Iffan smiled.

'If you've finished with your eating and drinking then come with me,' said Iffan, getting up to leave.

'Saheb, the tea is just coming,' said K.P.

'Ikhtidaar can have it.'

'Saheb, that bill is also just coming,' said K.P.

'That won't come.'

Iffan paid the bill and left with Topi. Both were extremely happy. But both kept their secret to themselves and both began digging into their memory pool. Neither, however, could come up with anything worth talking about.

The point is that these two were separated before the nation became independent.

'Your Daadi must be very upset with Hindi becoming the national language?'

'She's dead.'

'Arre?'

'What arre? How long could she live?'

'But she was your Daadi.'

'My Daadi died on the day that I was buying bananas from Pancham's shop. I changed my Daadi that day. How's Abbu?'

'He passed away.'

'Baaji?' Topi did not say 'arre' but asked another question instead.

'Baaji left for Pakistan.'

'Munna?' Even this answer did not shock Topi.

'Munna is here. So is Munni.'

The conversation ended. Both fell silent. Both became sad. There was an invisible wall between them. The sound of their heartbeats could not be heard across this barrier.

'Could we not have managed without Pakistan?' Topi made the first move to hammer against the wall.

'Don't know,' said Iffan.

'And now I cannot even abuse Pakistan.'

'Why?'

'Baaji's gone there, *na*'.

'What does her husband do?'

'He's a Flight Lieutenant in the Pakistan Air Force,' said Iffan. 'Abbu was ill and the poor things could not get permission to come here. Baaji, too, could not come.'

'Why didn't you go?'

'I wanted to convince myself that I was not afraid of the Hindus.'

'How have the Hindus harmed your life? Did the Hindus stop your brother-in-law from coming here?'

'That's not the point.'

'Fir what's the point?'

'Not "fir", it's "phir".' Iffan corrected him angrily, grinding his teeth. Topi laughed out heartily. Several walls came crumbling down. Several fears evaporated. Several kinds of loneliness were left behind.

'The Language Improvement Programme is still going on,' said Topi. 'Yaar, what wonderful days those were, Bhai.'

'Yes.'

Both grew solemn again. Iffan was scared of the Hindus and so he hated them. Topi had fallen in love with ancient Indian culture, so he hated the Muslims—but both became sad. When the old sense of friendship climbed up the wall of hatred to peep out a little, both became sad. The past whizzed before them in a few seconds. All their talk, all those thoughts, all those slogans . . . both journeyed through the past events again and both felt disheartened with the thought that both were losers. When two shadows found themselves alone in the jungle of hypocrisy, they clung to each other.

'This University of yours—I can't make any sense of it.'

'Now see if you can make any sense of my wife.'

Iffan's drawing room was a largely plain one. The walls were naked. Over the artificial fireplace was a bust of Shankar. And close to the bust were two photographs in a nickel frame. One was of Iffan's Daadi's and the other was of Iffan's Abbu's.

'Have you snared Shankar thinking him to be Bhola?'

'The Gomati mingles with the Ganga, doesn't it?' said Iffan, smiling. 'I hate the Hindus but I love Shankar because He is exactly like human beings. Stupid. He was only one among many present when the ocean was being churned. But then he drank the poison alone. Why did he not give all those who took the nectar a spoonful of poison to taste? Maybe one has to take poison all alone. Maybe, this is the difference between human beings and God. Poison is consumed by Shiv, alone. Socrates drinks poison, alone. Christ carries his cross, alone. Only one Prince is able to renounce the world. There is never a crowd at the moment of a test. Maybe, at best, seventy or seventy-two people get together at Karbala. Why is man always alone, Balbhadra?'

'Because this is his lunch time,' said Sakeena, coming into the room.

'This is my wife, Sakeena.'

'Even I could guess this much.'

'Don't laugh at the way he speaks,' said Iffan. 'His family speaks Urdu. He remains an illiterate at the behest of his Daadi.'

'That's not the truth at all, Bhabi.'

'Then what's the truth?' asked Sakeena. Her eyes sparkled with mischief.

'This is my childhood friend, Balbhadra Narayan Shukla.'

'Couldn't you have had a simpler name?' asked Sakeena.

'He is a typically staunch Hindu. Does not eat food touched by a miyaan. Or have you changed now?' Iffan asked Topi.

'Oh, this is good news,' said Sakeena. 'Actually, at this moment, I don't exactly have food suitable for the illiterates.'

This talk hurt Topi. And so he decided to give in to Sakeena's demands and eat there.

That was the first time that he ate in a Muslim home. After coming to Aligarh, he had lost the habit of eating from a plate. Yet he found it strange to pour soup from the same serving bowl that Iffan ate from. It was not an easy thing at all to take dal from the same ladle that Sakeena used to take dal for herself. His hands trembled many a time and drops of soup and dal fell on the tablecloth. But he did not lose heart. The dal had a new taste too. It was the first time that he was having *moong* dal with fried garlic, for, in his house, onions and garlic were taboo. In his house, dal would have a watery consistency and ghee would be mixed into it. That was quite delicious, but Sakeena's dal fry too had a taste all its own.

'Now don't ever ask me to eat here,' Topi said after he had finished eating.

'Why?' Sakeena's beautiful eyebrows became tense.

'Arre Bhai, explain this to her,' Topi told Iffan. 'I am a very staunch Hindu.'

'I too am a very staunch Muslim,' said Sakeena. 'After you leave I will scrub these utensils hard.'

'So if I had not eaten these utensils would not have been scrubbed neat? This is why I say that Muslims are dirty,' said Topi.

Sakeena gritted her teeth, at a loss for a fitting reply.

This is how Sakeena and Topi met for the first time at the lunch table and in their very first meeting, quarrelled.

IX

Now, all that you know about Sakeena is that she is Iffan's wife. But she was not born as Iffan's wife.

She was born as an only daughter in a very well-to-do Muslim household. She was the only sister to three brothers.

This is how it was before Pakistan was created, because after Pakistan there was only one brother.

Sayyed Aabid Raza was a famous lawyer of Chhapra and came from a good family. He was Naqvi Sayyed. His 'Sayyedness' was as crisp as newly printed currency notes. He maintained that his honour depended on his lineage more than on his wealth.

Sayyed Aabid Raza belonged, like a family inheritance did, to the Congress Party. This was the third generation that was attached to the Congress. His father had been a leader of the local community and been jailed several times. He himself was a Secretary in the Zilla Committee and, all put together, he must have spent some nine years, eight months, and twelve days in jail. He had worn nothing but *khaadi* all his life. And this khaadi he wore was of the really coarse variety. Now there is no need to specifically mention that he was a strong opponent of the Muslim League brand of politics. All his four children (Sakeena and her three older brothers) were integral parts of his soul. All three of his sons were against Pakistan. All three had studied in Aligarh and were called Communists. Time and again they were beaten up by members of the Muslim Students' Federation and by Muslim goons. However, they continued to oppose Pakistan. But when P.C. Joshi's Communist party decided to join hands with the Muslim League in 1945, it embittered all the three brothers.

The eldest brother even mentioned that if the League wished to use Muslims as mere exhibit pieces then it might as well directly use the Pakistan Zindabad slogan. And thank you comrades, you are welcome to use this slogan. . . . .

He was so disgusted that he left politics for good and joined his father in his legal practice.

In the elections of 1945, Aabid Raza stood on the Congress ticket. He lost his deposit. That he lost his deposit was not an ordinary event. For, even among the Muslims, he was a very revered person. But in those days the Muslims had to decide whether Pakistan would come to exist or not. The ordinary Muslims did not know that even if a Pakistan came to be, it would not be in Chhapra. They did not know that if they wished to go to Pakistan they would have to first destroy their dear Chhapra. The ancient homes, the communities, the timeless lanes and by-lanes, and fields—they would have to leave all these behind. Had they known this then, perhaps Sayyed Aabid Raza would not have lost his deposit. Then perhaps, maybe, he would not have been garlanded with slippers. Then perhaps he would not have been derided as a slave of the Hindus: 'Will you people vote for that Sayyed Aabid Raza who plays *Holi*? Will you give your votes to that Sayyed Aabid Raza whose daughter, each year, ties *raakhis* to two unknown Hindus? If your Islamic self-respect is dead, then for sure go ahead and vote for him. But ask yourself, how will you be able to face Aan Hazat (*Paigambar*) on the Day of Judgement? I admit that Sayyed Aabid Raza is an extremely learned person. I admit too that Pehalwaan Abdul Gaffoor Saheb is illiterate. But I know this too that Aan Hazat ignored all the Arab scholars and chose the unlettered Bilaal Razi Allah Taala Anho from Habash to be the muezzin caller in his Masjid. Whom will you support? The illiteracy of Bilaal or the scholarship of Abbu Jehal?'

When a young man from Aligarh raised these questions, the Muslims of Chhapra were carried away by his arguments. And they decided to elect Pehalwaan Abdul Gaffoor to be the 'muezzin caller' at the Assembly.

Even at this juncture, Sayyed Aabid Raza tried to explain to them: 'I know that you will be voting for Pehalwaan. But I am fighting for a principle, for a cause. . . .' This was when the first shoe hit him. 'Thank you. What I was telling you was that the Muslim League is a sham. . . .'

'Hindu dog *hai-hai*!' shouted the crowd.

'I am not Paigambar,' said Aabid Raza. 'People have thrown muck even at him. . . .'

'You dare to compare yourself with Aan Hazat?' An excited young man stood up. People in the crowd and the Congress workers were outnumbered. And when Sayyed Aabid Raza recovered consciousness, it was to find himself in hospital.

That day Sakeena abused Jinnah to her heart's content.

When she reached close to where her father's and two of her brothers' dead bodies lay, she recalled each one of her abuses. She heard, once again, the announcement of the dates for the election. Your attention friends, your attention friends . . .

Mahesh had pleaded with Sayyed Aabid Raza that these were the days of riots; that he should come and stay with them. Anything could happen at any time here. Sakeena tied raakhis to Mahesh, and Mahesh's father was one of Sayyed Saheb's closest friends.

'Have I been opposing the Muslim League so that when India becomes independent I should come to your house for refuge?' asked Sayyed Saheb.

'Chachaji, we can always discuss this later,' said Mahesh.

'No, son! This is the right time to discuss this issue.'

'At least send Sakeena away from here.'

But Sayyed Aabid Raza was not willing to do this either. It was just a few days ago that he had got her married. She now belonged to Iffan.

'I have written to them to send someone to come and take Sakeena with them. There is no rioting in Lucknow.'

But all three sons were adamant and Sakeena was sent to Mahesh's house. When Mahesh was returning after bringing Sakeena home, he was murdered on the way. Meer Saheb did not get the news of Mahesh's murder. Though he continued to get reports of other people's deaths.

The situation in the city went from bad to worse. Everyone was lonely. Familiar streets crawled like snakes; their hoods open, they were waiting to see footprints. The sounds of footsteps had changed—everyone walked rapidly. Eyes had sprouted on every shoulder and every back. Shadows had become Hindus and Muslims and everyone was running away, afraid of his own shadow. Tiny shards of shattered dreams pricked his feet like broken pieces of glass. But he could not scream in pain. He was scared. What if someone heard him scream? What if someone found out the street where he was hiding?

Man.

Human beings.

Both words have the same meaning. Yet the sounds of these two words clashed with each other. Mahesh was a human being. Men murdered him. Sayyed Aabid Raza was a man. Human beings killed him.

The third son was in Delhi. Both sons tried explaining a great deal to their father that these were not the days to step out of the house. But

Sayyed Aabid Raza said: 'These are the very days when one should step out of the house, son!'

'Abba, why don't you try to understand?' The elder son was annoyed. 'You don't seem to understand, son,' said Sayyed Aabid Raza. 'Have I spent my days in jail for this? You people can only get killed. But in the hamlets of Hindustan and Pakistan, my spirit is being stripped. My dreams are being raped and violated. You did not wear the garland of shoes. And those who garlanded me with shoes were not strangers. So does that mean that they were right? It is important to get the answer to this question. And to get the answer to this question I have to get out of the house.'

So he got out of his house. That same long *achkan*. That same black Irani topi. Elder son to his right. Younger son to his left. Babu Gaurishankar saw them from the window of his house.

'Sayyed Saheb!' he screamed.

Something like a crowd was coming towards them. Gaurishankar Babu leaped out of his house with a gun. But the game was over before he could reach the spot. Sayyed Aabid Raza's Irani topi rolled limply and fell into the gutter.

'Do you know who he is?' Gaurishankar Babu shook one of the young fellows and asked him. 'This is Sayyed Aabid Raza.'

Gaurishankar was of the opinion that this name would work some kind of magic and the topi lying in the gutter would fly and settle automatically on Sayyed Saheb's head and he would stand up, smiling. But nothing of that sort happened. The topi remained where it was, in the gutter.

'The way you say his name Aabid Raza as if he were some God.'

'No, no. You are the God.'

Babu Gaurishankar returned home, his head hung low. The youth he had shaken up belonged to the same locality.

The news that Aabid Raza had been killed spread like forest fire. Chhapra was shrouded in silence. Rioting stopped. This was the answer to Aabid Raza's question. The answer to Aabid Raza's question was also this that Gaurishankar Babu stood witness against that youth. The answer to Aabid Raza's question was Mahesh's dead body.

But Sakeena could only remember those abuses that she had hurled at Pakistan. The next year, she did not tie a raakhi on Ramesh, Mahesh's brother. She bought a raakhi. But an Irani topi seemed to peep out of that raakhi. Throwing the raakhi into the gutter, she sat down to write a letter to the brother who had gone away to Pakistan directly from Delhi.

. . . Why should I tie a raakhi on Ramesh bhaiyya? What can I do—Iffan won't agree to come to Pakistan. I've begun to hate this country . . .

Hatred!

This is such a strange word! Hatred! This single word is the product of the national movement for Independence. The price of the dead bodies of revolutionaries in Bengal, Punjab, and Uttar Pradesh is just one word— hatred!

Hatred!

Suspicion!

Fear!

We are crossing the river on these three floats. These three words continue to be sowed and reaped. These are the words that flow as milk from the mother's breast and into the child's gullet. From behind the crevices of the locked doors of people's hearts, these are the three words that peep out. Like homeless spirits, these three words buzz around in the open courtyards. They beat their wings like bats and hoot like owls in the stillness of night. They cross our paths like the proverbial black cats. Like pimps, they incite and abet quarrels and like hooligans, they tease those with virgin dreams and kidnap them in broad daylight.

Three words! Hatred, Suspicion, Fear. Three demons.

'I hate every Hindu,' said Sakeena.

'You are doing a very sensible thing,' said Topi. ' Now Bhai will not be suspicious about you and me. And by the way, I too am not specially fond of the Muslims.'

'Then why do you come here?'

'This house belongs to a friend of mine.'

Friend.

Oh, so this word still exists, does it?

X

✦

Topi was a second child. He had become used to being shouted at, to wearing clothes handed down to him from Munni Babu, to giving in to Bhairav's tantrums. In Aligarh, there was no one to shout at him. Nor was there anyone to tell him what he should or shouldn't do. That was why, even after initially making a few friends and then later on making a lot of friends, he continued to feel lonely. This was a serious situation indeed.

When he met Iffan, he got a second lease of life. And when Sakeena shouted at him at their very first meeting, he felt as if quenched of a thirst that had been growing in him for over two years. He started spending almost all his time in Iffan's house. He would come over irrespective of whether Iffan was at home or not. He would rummage through Iffan's books, get shouted at by Sakeena, would try to teach Hindi to five-year-old Shabnam, and in return get shouted at by Sakeena again. . . .

His visits to Iffan's house became so frequent that this became the topic of conversation at Shamshad Market, at the Staff Club, at Café de Fuse, and at Café de Alaf Laila!

The University is a small community. Very different from a city. Several people at the University even forget that Muslims are a majority in Pakistan! That beyond the bridge is Hindustan. On this side of the bridge is the University. That is why people are busy keeping track of other people's movements. Whose wife smiles at whom, which boy is now having an affair with which girl, and who is he likely to fall for next. . . .

Sex.

Frustration.

Fanaticism.

'Maulana Muhammad Ali used to live in this room.'

'Hasrat Mohani, Liaqat Ali, Sadar Ayyub, Lala Amarnath, Ghouse Muhammad, Shaqur, Talat Mehmood—is there anyone who hasn't studied here!'

'Aligarh University is the name of a culture.'

'All of them must have had a great time here.'

'Anyone who hasn't studied here is an illiterate.'

'Here even the uncivilized acquire finesse.'

'Look at that creep Nargis. Broke away from Raj Kapoor only to hang on to Sunil Dutt.'

'What a catch Topi, too, has found!'

'Look at the times—so many Muslim girls are getting married to Hindu boys.'

'Whenever lightning strikes it always falls on the poor Muslims.'

'Anyone else would have been a better choice than Topi, Bhai. Come on, let's go, that's the muezzin's call.'

Iffan did not bother much with what he heard. Sakeena started to go to the movies with Topi, but Topi was unable to accept this slander. He said: 'Bhai, this University of ours has turned out to be such a horrible lowly place.'

'Why?'

'Now I won't come here anymore.'

'Why? Are you having an affair with Sakeena?'

'Only this *Kaalicharan* is left for me now,' said Sakeena.

'Uncle Topi, you . . .' began Shabnam.

'Beware—don't call me Topi again/"fir".'

'Topi, for Allah's sake don't ruin my child's tongue,' Sakeena entreated earnestly.

'Why should I do anything for your Allah's sake?' asked Topi. 'Arre, I have sent Him away to Pakistan.'

'Uncle Topi is a Hindu.' Shabnam said this clapping her hands in a manner that implied that only fools could be Hindus.

'Who told you this?'

'Today a friend of mine was telling me in school that Ammi is having an affair with Topi. And that Topi Uncle is a Hindu.' Shabnam started clapping again. 'You are a Hindu.' She repeated the abuse.

There was a stunned silence in the room. Topi's face went red with anger. Iffan grew sad. Sakeena burst into laughter.

'People here do not even know how to malign you properly,' said Sakeena. 'I'm sure listening to such stories will just give Topi some strange ideas. He might go and propose to some girl and get beaten with shoes.'

'It's Raksha Bandhan today. Why don't you tie me a raakhi?'

Raakhi!

Mahesh. Ramesh.

Raakhi!

'I don't tie raakhis on Hindus.'

'Shreemati Jargaam, only Hindus tie raakhis.'

'If you mispronounce my husband's name, I'll kill you.'

'Uncle is a Hindu,' Shabnam whispered into her doll's ears.

'But . . .'

'Just stop your but "gut".' Sakeena was now getting irritated. 'Should I tie you a raakhi just because the gossip mongers here are trying to malign me? I buy a raakhi every year and throw it into the gutter.'

'And you forget that Mahesh risked his life to save you. And that Ramesh continued to travel miles to come to your house to get the raakhi tied,' said Iffan.

'Yes. But I cannot forget that Abba's Irani topi was flung into a gutter.'

'Oh, come on, did I throw your Abba's topi into the gutter?' asked an annoyed Topi.

'Just shut up. You too are a Hindu.'

'What kind of logic is this? Ok. So now you throw me into a gutter. I am also a "topi". That will even out things.'

Sakeena got up from her place. Iffan pretended to browse through a book. Topi got restless. There was no point trying to engage these Muslims in a dialogue!

'Bhai, take this wife of yours and go away to Pakistan.'

Iffan did not reply. He was lost in thought. He thought that if there had been a Muslim in Topi's place then perhaps the people would not have gossiped so much.

That same Hindu business again!

Will this word continue to chase them?

Topi, why are you a Hindu? Or why am I a Muslim? Why? This 'why' too is such a strange word. It forces people into manufacturing answers. But what if we do not find the answer? What should we do then?

Iffan flung the book aside.

'You hate the Muslims. Sakeena abhors the Hindus. I . . . I am scared perhaps. Where will all this lead to Balbhadra? My fears and the hatred in your heart and Sakeena's—are these such fixed truths that they just cannot change? What will the history teacher teach shortly? What sort of an explanation will he provide of a situation where I was afraid of you and you hated me. And despite this we were friends. Why don't I murder you? Why don't you kill me? Who is it that stops us? I cannot teach History. I'll put in my resignation.'

'This will not be a very wisdom thing to do.'

'But . . .'

'Bhai.' Topi interrupted him. 'Why did you not correct me when I used the word wisdom?'

Iffan smiled.

Both fell silent. There was nothing to be said. For the first time Iffan questioned his fears. And for the first time Topi was perplexed by his hatred. What was untrue—the friendship or the fear? Friendship or hatred . . . ?

'Then why do the Muslims not get jobs?' Iffan asked this question as if it were in continuation of a long-drawn debate on the Hindu-Muslim problem.

'Because their hearts are filled with guilt,' said Topi.

'What guilt?'

'The guilt that now that they have made their Pakistan they cannot really claim a right to India. Bhai, in every Muslim's mind there is a window that opens out towards Pakistan.'

'Then why did I not go to Pakistan?'

Topi had no answer to this question. Come to think of it, why had this Iffan not gone to Pakistan? Why had four or four-and-a-half crore Muslims stayed back in India? Why has my neighbour Kabeer Mohammed built a new house . . . ?

'But why do the Muslims celebrate when the Pakistan hockey team wins a match?'

'We could ask this question differently—why is it that in the Indian hockey team there are no Muslims? Have the Muslims forgotten to play hockey?'

'No, but there is this constant fear that they will join hands with the Pakistani side.'

Fear!

So, this fear exists on both sides! The sadness deepened further. Darkness increased. Where all does this fear exist? Is there any possibility of getting rid of this fear?

'How can the Muslims prove that they will not join hands with the other side if they are never allowed to play against the Pakistanis?'

'We cannot forego our gold medal just to test how loyal the Muslims are, can we?'

'Then what is the solution?'

'Supposing it is not hockey but war. If we recruit Muslims into the army to test their loyalty and if they join hands with the Pakistanis, then who will have to pay the price for this test?'

This logic pleased Topi. It was better to continue to be suspicious. It was good to continue with the hatred. If the worst came to the worst, there would be riots. A hundred, or maybe twice that number of people, would die . . .

'Just to save the lives of a hundred or two hundred people we cannot jeopardize our independence, can we?'

'Then?'

'Then what? Have I taken on the responsibility of looking after the Muslims?'

Topi was filled with anger. He made Iffan the target of his anger. If Iffan had not been a Muslim then he would not have been bothered by such troublesome questions.

This question does not leave us alone. Man might defeat death, but he cannot vanquish some fundamental doubts. Some question or the other will always remain to nag us . . .

'If the Muslims are so bad then why have you come to their University to study?' asked Iffan.

'Does this University belong to the father of the Muslims?' asked Topi. 'The aid that it gets from the regional government—doesn't our money go into that fund? All Muslims are traitors.'

'Yes.' Sakeena entered the room. 'My Abba too was a traitor, wasn't he?'

'Why do you keep dragging your Abba into every conversation? As if he were, not Abba, but Ram. Omnipresent. Many other abbas also died during the riots,' Topi screamed. He suddenly realized what he had said. 'Sorry Bhabi.'

He got up in a hurry and left.

While leaving he even forgot to kiss Shabnam. Usually, he would kiss Shabnam and she would quickly wipe her cheeks out of fear that his black colour would make a patch on her skin.

'Why didn't Uncle Topi kiss me?' Shabnam asked her mother.

'He's gone mad.'

The next day Shabnam told her friends in school that her Ammi had said that Uncle Topi had gone mad.

Her friends told this to their respective mothers and the wheel of gossip turned again.

XI

✦

News spread all over the University that Sakeena had refused to tie Topi a raakhi. Some people praised Sakeena for her courage—that she did not make Topi her brother just to save face. Shame on Topi for going to his beloved and asking her to 'tie him a rakhi.'

'*Yadi* (if) you have not told this, who could have let this out?' Topi asked Sakeena. 'Who else knew about this?'

'Look here, don't use this "yadi padi" in my presence, understand? Illiterate fool.'

'Amazing. You are never tired of praising me enough for my language —your best wishes seem to be unending.' Then he spoke gently. 'Listen, Bhabi, this is a serious matter. Ask Bhai.' He turned towards Iffan. 'Why don't you tell her Bhai? After studying in this University I am now not fit for any other University. If this scandal continues, you think I'll ever get a job here?'

'I thought you were worried about *my* reputation getting spoiled,' said Sakeena.

'These days safeguarding a job is no less important than safeguarding a reputation.'

'So as long as you get your job you don't mind if I get slandered?'

'As long as your husband does not suspect you why should you worry?' asked Topi. 'The question, however, is—how did this raakhi business get out of the house?'

The next day even this conversation got out of the house. And when in Rahmat's teashop a few boys started teasing Topi, Topi lost his head.

'Why are you jealous?' asked Topi angrily.

The problem was that the boy to whom Topi said these words was a minor good-for-nothing bully. He immediately drew up his sleeves. Topi did not know how to hit back or fight. He was soundly beaten up.

The local newspapers highlighted the episode. And Iffan started losing his credibility at the University. Everyone agreed that he was a scholar and a learned person. All agreed that he even taught conscientiously. But if a teacher's wife was involved with a student then what was the point of all his learning. That is why word went round the University quite openly that he would never become a Reader. What happened as a result was that Dr Suhail Qadri's stock began to go up.

'Whatever's happening to Dr Zargaam is absolute injustice.' Around the bridge table at the Staff Club one evening, Dr Qadri said, 'What has the University got to do with his personal life? Even assuming that whatever is being said about him is true, where is it laid down that a teacher's wife . . .'

'Four no trumps,' called out his partner.

'No.'

'Five clubs.' Dr Qadri was lost in his game.

When Iffan's chances of becoming a Reader seemed so threatened, what chance did Topi have of ever getting a lecturer's post? And so the chances of Anwar Mujtaba Zaidi and Ramvilas 'Bekhatak' brightened in the Hindi Department.

Mr Anwar Mujtaba Zaidi was junior to Bekhatakji. Bekhatakji had submitted his thesis and Mr Zaidi's thesis had got stolen! But Zaidi Saheb claimed that since Aligarh University was the only Muslim University, he had a greater right to the post. If all the jobs in Hindustan went to the Hindus, couldn't one Muslim University belong completely to the Muslims?

Jobs!

It used to be told that in the past young men dreamt of conquering nations, of undertaking long and arduous journeys, of bringing honour to the family. Now they only dream of getting jobs! Getting a job is the biggest adventure of this generation! The Fahiyaans and the Ibn-Batutas, the Vasco da Gamas and Scotts are today busily engaged in searching for jobs. The single aim of the Christs, the Mohammeds, and the Rams of today is to get a job!

Jobs! This word of four letters and one syllable is the ultimate test of today's dreams. Those who pass this test are the realized souls. Homes and families grow only when there are jobs. Anwar Mujtaba Zaidi's marriage was precariously dependent on his job.

Zaidi was in love with his father's younger brother's daughter, Bilqis Fatima. Bilqis Fatima too loved him just as intensely. The uncle too did not wish to send his daughter away to Pakistan, although he continued to get very good proposals for his daughter from there. But if Mujjan miyaan (Anwar Mujtaba Zaidi) did not get a job, then he would be forced to find a match for his daughter in Pakistan.

In earlier times it used to be the emperor who stood between two loving hearts. Now it is a job. Like everything else, the worth of love, too, has deteriorated considerably.

> . . . What can I say? These Hindu fanatics have made it impossible for us to live here. If the Head of my Department had been a Muslim I would have without doubt got this job. But Billo, don't lose heart. I will definitely get a job, if not here then somewhere else. The independence of Hindustan has been the cause of so much trouble.

When Bilqis received this letter she felt very sad, for she had read in books that Laila never gets her Majnu and that Sheeri never gets her Farhaad. She started making a plea at every namaaz. O Pure One, please bring a change of heart in that idiot of a Head. There is nothing that You cannot do . . .

Her pleas perhaps never reached The Pure One or else The Pure One did not particularly pay attention to her pleas for, neither Topi nor Anwar Mujtaba Zaidi got the job. Bekhatakji was selected.

To top it, Doctor Qadri became a Reader.

And furthermore, a Pakistani match was settled for Bilqis.

Bekhatak was congratulated by whoever he met. No one asked, 'Bhai, how did this happen? Isn't Topi more qualified than you?' In our country, the proof of being qualified lies in getting a job. That is why no one told Zaidi, 'What do you think you are doing? Can't you see Bekhatak is more qualified than you are?' Well, at the University no one pays any attention to scholarship.

This 'job' factor is quite a killer. Experts who come from outside are interested in their 'allowances' and are in a hurry to board the next train. It is the Head of the Department who makes the selections, all by himself. And he has his likes and dislikes. He chooses only those whom he likes. And sometimes he is not able to do even this as there are a thousand other pressures working upon him.

'Now I can't even say that I did not get the job because I am a Hindu,' said Topi. 'Bhai, my love for your wife has left me with nothing.'

'And my love for you has left me with nothing,' said Iffan.

'So come, let's start a Union of "Depheated" Lovers.'

'A union of Defeated Lovers!' said Iffan gritting his teeth.

'God! Even now you are bothered about the language!'

Iffan laughed.

'And I haven't yet told you the news of this century,' said Topi.

'Have you got a job somewhere else?' asked Sakeena eagerly.

'Now where would I get a job from!' said Topi. 'My scholarship has been detained.'

'In a jail?' asked Shabnam.

'Yes.'

'Then he must have robbed something?'

'This is absolutely absurd!' said Iffan.

'What is so absurd about this?' asked Topi. 'The University was giving me the scholarship. It has now stopped giving it.'

'But why?' asked Sakeena.

'Because I am your *aashiq* (lover).'

Topi pulled out the 'sh' from 'aashiq' with great panache.

'Uncle, what does aashiq mean?'

'It means that I am in love with your mother,' said Topi.

'That's what Sister Alema too was saying.'

'Really?'

'Yes.'

'Do please tell that Sister Alema of yours that I love her too.'

'But she's so horrible.'

Yet, Shabnam did carry Topi's message to Sister Alema. And then an amazing thing happened. Sister Alema forgot how to speak in English! She started crying in the classroom. The girls were stunned and wondered what had come over Sister. More than being taken aback by her tears, they were surprised by the Urdu she started speaking.

Sister lodged a complaint with Mother Superior.

'I'll commit suicide,' she said, sniffing and wiping her nose.

Mother Superior phoned the Vice-Chancellor. The Vice-Chancellor phoned the Proctor. The Proctor issued a summons for Topi. And news spread all over the University that Topi was actually in love with Sister Alema.

Sister Alema went to her room and wiped her tears, after which she stood in front of the mirror. She was bored with what she saw in front of her. Dark face, small dirty eyes. Smallpox marks. A long jar-like neck. Firm pointed breasts. Whenever she saw her breasts she would always feel shy and quickly cover herself with her duppatta.

This was the first stone of slander ever cast at her. God knows for how long she had waited for this kind of a recognition. On being hit by this stone, her listless body suddenly became energized.

That very moment she moved towards the Department of English to speak with Miss Zaidi. For the first time she saw the faces of the girls around her with great love—the slightly plain ones, the beautiful ones, the ugly ones and the indifferent ones. She could now empathize with all those girls with whom no one fell in love and who therefore said things like—Hai Allah Majid Bhai, oh come on Hakim Bhai you actually scared me . . . and things like that. There was this girl in her very hostel, Qamar. She would read out a poet's letter to all the girls. He's written this, he's written that. . . . He's sent me this sari for my birthday. . . . All the girls envied her and wondered why the poet did not write them any letters. And one day, Qamar's lie was out in the open. She used to write those letters herself. When this lie was out, the girls started talking about their affair with the same poet in her presence. The poor girl ran off to her home and the rumour mills here spread the story that she had gone off to abort the baby. She never returned. Alema decided that today she would write Qamar a letter. She had heard from 'sources' that Qamar had been married to a 'big officer' from Pakistan. How is it that there are so many big officers in such a small country? India is such a big country. Girls here don't manage to find even clerks!

'Hello,' said Miss Zaidi. 'I am so sorry about all these things that are being said. This is the limit, I say. . . .'

Right through the day, Sister Alema went around gathering sympathy.

The fact is that in an environment like the one in the Muslim University, there can only be this hypocritical or depraved variety of love. Girls are sent here so that when other girls go back home they can talk about them. That is why the girls always remain alert. They keep looking here and there, all around them, taking care to see that they are not caught watching. In these matters the 'professional brothers' prove very helpful. These 'brothers' keep changing their sisters. This matter is however never carried beyond a point. At best, a couple of films are seen. Or there's a picnic at the fort. A few small gifts are exchanged. A hand accidentally touches the other's hand. Some imagined fluff is brushed from the other's eyes, a few letters written or arranged to be written. If this matter builds up further, then a few female friends here are told of the secret and a few male friends there are kept informed. Sometimes the matter grows beyond this as well. When that happens, a 'sister' starts dreaming in a room here and some 'brother' does the same in his room there. Before the dreams can reach their rightful destinations, it is time for exams. And during exam times where else can you find love blossoming except in Indian films?

The *Crooked Lines* of Ismat Chugtai have not yet become straight.

Sister Alema too had been sent to Aligarh for this very reason—that some brother of some sister would select her. This however did not happen. Now would there be a sister who would choose a dark squint-eyed, pock-marked Sister Alema for her brother? Younger girls were chosen and these girls even got married. While Sister Alema remained where she was—like an untouched utensil.

Alema was very fond of speaking in English. That is why she was called Sister Alema from the time that she had been in High School. The height was that Mumtaaz *Aapa* (Principal, Girls' College), too, called her Sister Alema. And then when she became a part-time teacher in a Convent and worked directly under Mother Superior, who could stop her from being Sister Alema?

There was this special thing about Sister Alema. She never lost hope. That is why as soon as she got Topi's message her heart bloomed in a manner as if it had been touched by spring for the first time!

She could not sleep that night. Her heart ached for Topi. *Hai*, the poor fellow—hope he does not get rusticated. Wonder what came upon me, why did I go and make that complaint so unthinkingly?

(Sister Alema certainly spoke in English but whenever there was a need to think she did that only in her mother tongue.)

She got up in the morning feeling depressed.

'What happened? Didn't you sleep last night?' asked the person who stayed in the adjoining room.

'I did sleep, but saw such horrible dreams!'

'Dreams!' That girl laughed. 'Don't you start seeing dreams Sister Alema. When you see sweet dreams they turn out to be even more horrible!'

The girl who said this was called Mehnaaz. An ordinary looking girl. Had come of age five or six years ago. Was a lecturer. Whoever she fell in love with would always be hooked by another girl, leaving her alone again. Her latest lover, Dr Waheed, had just a few days ago married Dr Shaukat Farooqui—married Dr Miss Farooqui! (It is important to mention that Miss Farooqui was a woman.)

At the time that she was seeing Dr Waheed, all her friends were sure that this time the affair would lead to marriage. She, however, was never sure about this.

Doctor Waheed had quite a reputation with women. *Bas*, it only had to be a girl. His modus operandi too was quite simple. He was tired of his wife. He would speak of his family matters in a sombre tone and continuously puff away at his Charminars.

He employed the same tactic with Mehnaaz as well. Mehnaaz was Wajeeda's friend. She knew his lines by heart. She hated this doctor for he had broken the heart of a girl like Wajeeda. Yet, she was swept away by the waves of his sorrowful tone. And by the time she recovered enough to be alert, she realized that both of them had left the shores far behind.

That is why she was now afraid of dreams.

'I am not talking about those kinds of dreams,' said Sister Alema. There was so much passion in her voice that Mehnaaz was startled. She became even sadder.

'Who is this Topi?' asked the Sister.

'Doing his research in Hindi,' said Mehnaaz. 'And is caught up with that History teacher Zaidi Saheb's wife, Sakeena Zaidi.'

'Then how . . .' said the Sister and stopped.

Mehnaaz moved away. Sister Alema was left standing alone in the corridor. The walls of Sultaniya hostel suddenly became too high. Just like that. Exactly like the walls of the magical palaces in some magical films. Sister Alema used to hate such films. Yet she did become a princess for some time—a princess who had been kept captive by a magician in his magical palace. She began waiting for her prince. . . .

The prince himself was in great trouble. The Deputy Proctor, Mukhtaar Saheb was drilling him.

'So, you are in love with Sister Alema, is it?'

'Mukhtaar Saheb, the thing is that . . .'

'You did not even pause to think that she is so many years older than you?'

'There was no need for me to think about this because . . .'

'You are in love with her.' Mukhtaar Saheb interrupted Topi.

'You don't listen to what I have to say . . .' said Topi, getting angry.

'Go on, pour out the trash you want me to listen to.'

'Do you want me to hold Ganga water in my hands and say that I absolutely do not love Sister Alema? I do not even know her.'

'It will be difficult to order for Ganga water,' said Mukhtaar Saheb. 'Because the Ganga flows thirty miles from here. So tell us this, did you or did you not send a message to Sister Alema through Zaidi Saheb's daughter?'

'I had most certainly sent her a message. If Sister Alema has the right to say that I am in love with Bhabi . . . that is with Zaidi Saheb's wife, then I have the right to say that I am in love with her.'

'Have you come here to fall in love or to study?' Mukhtaar Saheb too started losing his temper. 'You are a senior student and so this first lapse on your part will be excused. You go apologize to Sister Alema. Miyaan, complete your Ph.D. and go home. You are getting spoilt in the company of the Communists.'

Topi left the Proctor's office in quite an angry state. What the hell was all this? That Sister Alema . . . what the hell does she . . .

By sheer chance, that very same day, he met Sister Alema for the first time in Ms Zaidi's house.

'Sister, tomorrow is Raksha Bandhan. I'll come over to your place. You could tie me a rakhi.'

The Sister was shocked.

The next day she applied for leave and went home never to return again. She had put in her resignation. Topi was teased about this incident for some time in the University. And then people forgot all about Sister Alema.

Sakeena met her in Shimla. There too she taught girls.

'How is Topi?' After inquiring about almost everyone at Aligarh, she gently asked this.

'Writing his thesis.'

'Still at it?'

'Arre, what can one do if one does not get a job? Instead of simply sitting at home it is better to go and do one's Ph.D.'

XII

✢

Topi was in trouble with the loss of his scholarship for Munni Babu had already become a politician. Bhairav too was doing well along the same lines. Frankly, this problem of unemployment has become so serious that the only thing every young person can dream of becoming today is a politician. Only one story inspired both Bhairav and Munni Babu. Bapu Gopinath was a mere bus conductor. Absolutely unlettered. Had a makeshift home. Then the magic wand appeared. He became an M.P. Now he owns a car, two bungalows, and two buffaloes. Has accounts in several banks. His son was studying for his engineering degree in America. His daughter had been married off with so much pomp that people talk about it to this day. The Collector greeted him— now what more can anyone ask for? So these two were not the slightest bit interested in the Blue Oil of Doctor Bhrugu Narayan.

Munni Babu and Bhairav, however, chose two different paths. Munni Babu loved the slogans on Hindu culture and tradition. What were these cow-killing Muslims, who worshipped a foreign God, doing here? If all these Muslims could be sent to Pakistan then their share of jobs would automatically come to the Hindus.

Jobs!

What a repulsive word!

Twice it so happened that the job that Munni Babu had applied for, went to a Muslim.

This thing called 'employment' is a double-edged sword. On the one hand it severs the Hindus from the Muslims and on the other, the Muslims from the Hindus. This country is just newly independent. So don't those boys whose fathers, uncles, distant Chachas, distant Mamas, (there aren't distant fathers—or are there?) . . . in short, any relative who had participated in the independence struggle—don't these boys have a greater right to employment? When these close and distant relatives were facing bullets, others were sitting comfortably at home. Or, if I am a member of a Commission, don't my relations or those of my caste and community have a greater right over all the jobs that come under my jurisdiction? These people around are fools. They don't understand these simple matters. That is why it is said, on the one hand, that the Congress is an enemy of the Muslims. The Congress rule is not secular or 'vecular' from any angle. It's a simple and straight Hindu rule. See for yourself. Muslims are never recruited to the police force or the army. If war breaks out our *dhoti*-clad heroes will flee at the sound of a cannon shot, clutching their *lotas* in their hands. It is also said that this Government is playing up to the Muslims while the general impression is that the Muslims are the agents of Pakistan. If there is war these people will move over to the other side.

Beards have sprouted in the hearts of Muslim boys and tufts in the hearts of Hindu boys. These boys study physics but do not write their answers without first marking 'Om' or 'Bismillah' at the top of the page.

'What's the point in learning science, Bhai?' said Topi bitterly. 'There needs to be a scientific temper too.'

'What's that?' asked Sakeena.

'Maybe he means a scientific attitude,' said Iffan.

'That's right,' said an already infuriated Topi. 'Keep sitting there, translating words.'

'Arre, what should I do then?' Iffan too was starting to lose his temper.

'You go on with your work, go on defending Aurangazeb. What else can you do?'

'Bhai, I had no hand in terminating your scholarship.'

'Your *Jouja* put an end to it.'

'Topi, for God's sake, don't you speak in Arabic-Persian, please,' Sakeena pleaded with folded hands. 'Jouja indeed! You could have said *beevi* instead.'

'My grandmother's soul has entered both of you,' said Topi. Then he turned towards Iffan. 'Do you know what's happening at the Union elections? The Jama'at boys are leading in Sahab Baug and V.M. Hall. There is a majority of Engineering and Science students in both these halls.'

'In Benares, who do the Engineering and Science students vote for?' asked Iffan. 'As far as I can remember, no Muslim boy has ever been elected even to the cabinet of the Benares University Union. Leave alone their major posts.'

'Bhai, this is a bad habit all of us at Aligarh have. Just pick up an issue and immediately the talk veers off to Benares University. Benares University is a Hindu University. All kinds of things can happen there. But here? Let me tell you, this Pakistani industry will not last for long.'

'Just listen to him!' Sakeena got agitated. 'Listen to this Hindu parrot, listen to the sounds he makes. This University is a Pakistani industry, is it?'

'What else is it then? If there is a Hindustan-Pakistan cricket match, these boys crowd into the mosque to offer prayers. The idiots don't even know that this territory does not come under Allah miyaan's jurisdiction. And even if it does, how can you pray for Pakistan's victory, Bhai? And then they'll sit and crib that they don't get jobs. That they are asked to give proof of their loyalty. We did this major thing in 1857, we did that in 1920. Please tell me you raconteurs, what the hell are you doing in 1960?'

'Go, go and ask them,' said Sakeena, blowing a kiss.

'Why the hell should I go and find out? Let the rascals die for all I care. I am going home tomorrow.'

'Why?'

'One, to coax my father. Will tell him that I have done my Ph.D. If I do my D.Litt. too then I'll have a double doctorate degree and then I can sell that Blue Oil. Doctor Balbhadra Narayan M.A., Ph.D., D.Litt. Illiterates will easily fall for such a string of degrees. Will earn enough money. My beloved father has not sent me a pie for the last six months. Then there is one more thing to be done. Municipal elections are about to be held there. Elder brother is standing on a Janasangh ticket. Younger on a Congress ticket. And so from today onwards I have become a Communist. I'll canvas on behalf of the Communist who counters these two. In some measure, I'll also be able to pay back the debt I owe to the Muslim University. The Communist there is a Muslim. And now I am quite fed up with my affair with Bhabi.'

Sakeena threw a cushion at Topi but it missed its target. Topi stood up. 'Now there is only one problem at hand.'

'No money to buy a ticket,' said Sakeena innocently.

'Yes.'

'I'm not giving you a single paisa.'

'But Bhabi, you will not be able to bear the thought of your brother-in-law being caught for ticketless travelling. The newspapers will carry the news of a student from the Muslim University—a Ph.D. and a prospective D.Litt. at that—caught for travelling without a ticket. Just think about the disgrace this will bring to your prestigious University.'

'I'll bear it.'

'Ok, then lend me the money.'

'You haven't yet returned the money you had borrowed earlier.'

'Will repay with interest. Let my father die or let me get a job.'

'Get married. Then you will have tonnes and tonnes of money.'

'There is already a moneyed daughter-in-law at home. Her face is like the political map of the pre-Chandragupt India. Thank you very much but I'll marry a non-moneyed woman.'

'Have you seen your own face?'

'I see it everyday. Would you have seven rupees? If you don't have seven, even ten or twenty will do.'

Sakeena knew that she would give him the money. Topi too knew that he would get the money. But it had become quite a regular practice with them to indulge in banter of this kind as a prelude.

The truth was that Sakeena and Topi had begun to grow very fond of each other. But Sakeena never tied him a raakhi. . . .

The compartment in which Topi sat was very crowded. Perhaps the crowd is the most remarkable identity-marker of the Indian Railways. Topi was wearing the black sherwani of the University.

'Let me finish my lunch and then you may sit,' said a Panditji who was eating and had his identity stamped on his face.

'Isn't it possible for you to carry on eating and for me to be seated?'

'You come and sit here son!' Panditji said this to a young man who was seated facing him. The man came there. 'You go and sit there,' Panditji told Topi.

'Why should I sit there?'

'Arre, then where do you wish to sit—on the Maharaj's head?' screamed a pot-bellied man.

'Is this Baba's head?' Topi banged his hands on the wooden berth.

'If you are so conceited then go to Pakistan,' spoke the pot-belly.

Topi understood the matter. He began to laugh.

'I'm sorry,' he apologized to Baba and sat on the adjacent berth. He sensed, however, that the people around were quite annoyed with him.

When Panditji finished eating, the pot-bellied man started talking with Panditji. Slowly, others around too were drawn into the conversation. There was a Muslim gentleman nearby.

'But Seth Saheb,' he said, 'just because I am a Muslim how does that prove that I am a Pakistani or that I am not prepared to be an Indian and live in this country?'

'Look at this gentleman here,' said the pot-belly, pointing towards Topi, 'he could clearly see that Baba was eating, but. . . .'

'I am a Hindu,' interrupted Topi. 'I am Balbhadra Narayan Shukla. And ok, let's assume that I am Sheikh Salamat—so what of it? These benches have been made so that travellers can sit on them. I wasn't snatching away Baba's food, was I? You are the people who push Muslims into the anti-India camp. Is this sherwani Muslim? This came in with Kanishka. These pajamas? These too came in at the time of Kanishka. . . .'

'This difference between the Hindus and the Muslims is a lie, son,' said the Panditji. 'It is God's grace that . . .'

'Why are you dragging poor God into this Panditji! I am a Hindu but I don't get a single job anywhere because I study in a Muslim University. You don't allow me to sit next to you because I am wearing a sherwani. And this pot-bellied gentleman is busy packing me off to Pakistan. Arre Baba, had I been a Muslim I would have myself stood at a distance on seeing you begin to eat. This person here is a Muslim. Look at him—he is so apologetic about being a Muslim! Poor thing is not even able to tell you, "look I too am an Indian citizen and who the hell are you to doubt my loyalty to this country?" One more layer of fear would have been deposited in his heart today. Now the next time he travels, he'll choose a compartment in which there are at least a fifteen or twenty other Muslims. And later, whenever anyone will tell him that Hindus will not allow Muslims to live in peace, he will recall this train journey. If you cannot eat in any of the ordinary compartments, then appeal to the government to run a few Hindu compartments where you can sit and eat in great comfort. Sri Ram can eat the *ber* fruit half-eaten by a *bheelni* but if I were a Muslim you will not allow me to even sit by your side. . . .'

Several thoughts began to race across the mind of this Muslim gentleman who sat close-by.

He was an educated man of around fifty or fifty-five. He too had nurtured fond dreams of Pakistan. He too had raised slogans. He was right in the forefront when Sayyed Aabid Raza of Chhapra was being garlanded with slippers. He had been a Commander of the Muslim National Guards. Several of his arguments kept coming back to him. He was a well-known small-time man. Whenever he stood up to make a speech, the whole gathering would be enticed by his arguments and slogans. He never said the namaaz. Never fasted during Ramzaan. Used to drink alcohol . . . but he stood up for the cause of the poor, downtrodden, exploited Muslims. And then Pakistan was born. He did not go to Pakistan. He became a Congressman! Became a member of the Zilla Committee. But beneath his khadi clothes, he still was a member of the Muslim League. He was on the look-out for an opportune moment.

Initially, he had toyed with the idea of going to Pakistan. But when he saw that leaders of every stature—small and big—were heading towards Pakistan, he changed his mind. What he declared to others was that unlike other opportunistic leaders he could not leave the Muslims to the mercy of the Hindus. In his heart of hearts, however, he was scheming to become a great leader. He had got two of his daughters married. They were happily settled in Pakistan. There was no Pakistani groom available for his third daughter and in any case . . . there was a dearth of eligible boys in India.

'. . . What if you had been born into a Muslim family? Does one have control over one's birth . . . ?' Topi's voice seemed to be coming from far away.

Malikzaada Abdul Waheed 'Tamanna' made a note of Topi's argument in the diary of his mind. He smiled. This boy does not know how to present an argument. He closed his eyes. A large gathering stood in front of him: 'I ask you this.' He heard himself say. (How he loved his own voice!) He thrust his fingers into the upper pocket of his sherwani. 'This is my question to you—if I am born into a Muslim family, is that my fault? Is there anyone here who can cross his heart and say that he willfully chose to be born into a particular community?' He paused, looked at the gathering, and smiled. The crowd took the cue and laughed . . .

'Sir, now you tell me!'

He started. Pot-belly was looking straight at him.

'Absolutely, yes, what else!' he said, spontaneously.

'Heard that?' The pot-belly told Topi.

Topi was perplexed. 'Are you saying that the heart of the majority of Muslims is preoccupied with Pakistan?'

Oh, so that was what was being discussed!

He smiled. 'Everyone's heart is preoccupied with Pakistan,' he said. 'Wasn't it, till yesterday, an integral part of our country? Why does man look towards the moon? Because he is a part of the earth. Yes, my heart is preoccupied with Pakistan because their senseless behaviour harms the interest of the Indian Muslims.' 'Tamanna' Saheb was quite pleased with his metaphoric use of the earth and the moon. He made a note of this example too in the diary of his mind.

The pot-bellied gentleman, Lala Nainsukh Prasad, was not ready for an argument of this sort because he had seen Muslims quake with fear whenever he had posed this question to them. That is why he studied this Muslim man rather carefully—the man who had countered his trap and managed to stand his ground, calmly, at a distance, smiling.

'Muslims are our brothers . . .' Lalaji began to say. 'All of us make mistakes. I am scared of these tensions that end in riots every day. Only a few die but then business comes to a standstill for months. . . .'

Topi started feeling nauseated. He knew that exactly like the Muslim sitting next to him, Lalaji too was telling lies.

He got up and walked towards the toilet. After that he kept looking out of the window. There was darkness everywhere. There was silence all around. Some light fell through the glass panes of the train. But the light never stayed on, as the train continued to move. A few things caught by the light could be seen momentarily, but soon the darkness would consume it. He got bored. The burden of the darkness all around him crept into his soul. Then a piece of darkness entered his eye. Rubbing that eye, he walked towards his seat.

The argument had ended. Lalaji's nose was speaking. Panditji had covered himself with a saffron coloured blanket and was already lying down. The Muslim traveller had allowed him to stretch his legs. Seated on the place meant for Topi, he was dozing.

As soon as he saw Topi, he stood up. It seemed as if he had been caught in the act of lying.

'No problem, you sit where you are,' said Topi to him. 'I'll sit in your place.'

'But . . .'

'I'll wake him up. I am not a Muslim.'

Panditji moved the blanket from his face.

'Keep your legs to yourself,' said Topi.

'Why?' asked Panditji. 'You sit in your place.'

'I'll sit somewhere else,' said the Muslim traveller.

'Why should you go somewhere else,' said an angry Topi. 'Will you go to Pakistan?'

The anger in Topi's voice put Panditji's legs in place. He sat up and in his heart of hearts started swearing at the Muslim traveller.

'Where are you going?' asked the Muslim traveller.

'Benares.'

'That's where I am going too.'

'Sure, do go.'

'Are you studying in the Muslim University?'

'Yes.'

'I, too, used to study there. I used to stay in 10, Morrison Court.'

'I too stay in that same room.'

This much was enough. The two became friends. They started talking about Aligarh. And then both started laughing about something. Lalaji opened his eyes.

'Which is-tation is this?' he asked, quite scared.

'There is no station here,' said Topi.

'Where are you going?'

'Home.' Then Topi went on. 'My father is a doctor. Of the Blue Oil fame. We are three brothers. One is married. Two aren't. My postal address is . . .'

'You Bhirgu Babu's son?'

'Yes.'

'Why these two—Munni Babu and Bhairav Babu fighting each other?'

'If not with each other then with whom should they fight?'

Lalaji burst into laughter at this question.

'You born standing?'

'Can't I stand so that the Panditji may sleep?'

Panditji pulled in his legs—they had slowly gone stretching towards Topi's waist.

'Doctor Saheb was being my classfellow. . . .'

Topi wanted to say something gritting his teeth, but he stopped himself. Was his father not enough that he had now to meet his father's class-fellows in railway compartments! He was afraid that if he did not silence Lalaji, there would be talk about his father right upto Benares. And now he could not even say that he was not the son of Doctor Bhrugu Narayan of the Blue Oil. He looked at the Muslim traveller with a great sense of helplessness.

'There will certainly be a war between Hindustan and Pakistan.' A voice came from the other end of the compartment. The ghost of politics spoke from the adjacent cabin. 'Then these miyaans will learn real lessons about life.'

'Do you know how many Muslims there were with Maharana Prataap in his fight against Akbar?' asked someone, 'and that all the letters written by Shivaji were in Persian? If Hindustan and Pakistan were to go to war then it would be the war of two nations, not of two religions.'

'Whatever be the reason for war, the miyaans will always side with Pakistan.'

'Who will the Hindus in Pakistan side with?' The question was asked. 'In the balance where loyalty is measured, there are two scales, mister!'

There was pin-drop silence.

'All Indian Muslims are Pakistani dogs.'

'Aren't you ashamed to call Hindustani human beings Pakistani dogs? Just by growing a tuft in the hair, man does not become God!'

'By adopting Islam man does not become the Prophet either. If you wish to live here then you must live here as a Hindu.'

'Then the Hindus there have to live as Muslims.'

'Our crops have failed.' A voice came from another cabin. 'Looks like God is unhappy.'

'Where are you from?'

'Baliya Zilla. Had gone in search of work. There is no work anywhere.'

'Hari . . . Ommm . . . Hari . . . Ommm.' The Panditji sitting close to Topi got up.

'If the Hindustan-Pakistan war is over, you may go to sleep.' Topi peeped into the next cabin to say this.

The other people in the cabin started laughing loudly and the Muslim traveller sitting in front of Topi breathed a sigh of relief.

XIII

During tea-time, the storm that was brewing all day, broke.

Topi reached home to find that both his brothers had gone out to make speeches at the election meetings. Doctor Saheb was in his shop. Ramdulari asked him to leave immediately and have a bath in the Ganga. What could he do? He went to his friend's house and had his bath there. Well, wasn't it water from the Ganga that flowed in the taps? Then where was the point in going all the way to the Ganga?

'So, which candidate are you going to support?' asked his friend, Vishambhar. He was a very strongly apolitical sort of person. He owned a cloth shop in 'Chitra'. This shop belonged, before him, to his father and before his father, to his grandfather. He believed that politics ruined business. What did a shop-owner have to do with politics? Chamaars, Muslims, Thakurs, . . . all were his customers. And what was a shop-keeper worth if he could not keep his customers happy? During election time, he promised to give his vote to anyone who asked for it. He professed to belong to the Jana Sangh and to the Muslim League. Several Muslim families were his customers right from his grandfather's times, two of whom had now gone away to Pakistan. Had Pakistan not been created, they would have continued to be his customers. This then was his political position. However, he felt it necessary to ask Topi which party he belonged to.

'I'll canvas for Kallan,' said Topi. Even a person like Vishambhar who had no definite political leanings was not prepared for this answer.

'Kallan?'

'Yes.'

Vishambhar burst out laughing. He was sure that Topi was being frivolous. But at home that evening, during tea-time, when the same conversation took place, no one thought that Topi was being frivolous. 'He has come from the Muslim University. He will work only for you,' Munni Babu told Bhairav pointing towards Topi.

'A lot of people who have not come from the Muslim University too are working for me,' said Bhairav. 'This is a matter of personal conviction! Please do not discuss your kind of politics with me. The Jana Sangh wants to push the country backwards.'

'And you want to harness the Muslims to your pair of bullocks to take this country forward? You will rest only after ruining Nehru's country. First it was Motilal, and then right from Sayyed Hassan's times, these Muslims have become the weakness of the Nehru family.'

'A lamp in a prostitute's room cannot light up an entire nation.'

Munni Babu was totally aghast on hearing this. He knew that the Congress loudspeakers raised politically correct slogans but what they whispered at his back was that Munni Babu would convert the Board into a centre for pimps and prostitutes. He had, however, never thought that of all persons Bhairav would say this—and that too so directly, to his face!

'Are you listening to all this, father?'

'Everybody is listening,' said Topi, 'and all of us have also heard what you have had to say.'

'I have said nothing wrong.'

'One doesn't know about that,' said Topi. 'But Bhairav is certainly saying the right thing. Your party is called the Jana Sangh (a people's party) and this party does not have a single office in a single village in this country. It should not have been named the Jana Sangh, bhaiyya—it should have been called the Baniya Sangh!'

'So, you have come all the way here to fight for Bhairav Babu's election, is it?' asked Munni Babu.

'No way, sir. I have come to canvas for Kallan's election.'

'That Muslim?' Munni Babu and Bhairav exclaimed.

'Bhairav Babu, why should you be bothered about the Hindu-Muslim question? You talk of secularism and socialism, don't you? Or have you become a Congressman purely for the sake of a ticket?'

'Now is that why you come here? To fight for miyaan election? Against your brothers? What is happening to this house?' Ramdulari became nearly hysterical. 'That is why I kept saying don't send him to Aligarh-"Uligarh".'

Ramdulari could not sleep that night. She could not understand how one brother could go against his other brothers—and that too for the sake of a miyaan?

Ramdulari did not understand politics. And she was not an enemy of the Muslims. She had picked up from here and there that some country called Pakistan had been formed. But what she got to know for sure from the Hindi newspapers was that the Muslims from across the border had done great injustice to the Hindus and this made her wary of the Muslims. That is why when Topi was being sent to Aligarh, she had opposed the idea vehemently. Ultimately, that which she feared most had happened. Topi had joined hands with the Muslims. As it is she was perplexed with the fact that Munni Babu and Bhairav never saw eye to eye over so many issues, and now Balbhadra! He had engineered a whole catastrophe. Anything could happen in *Kaliyug*! She had been wondering all the time that of her two sons who was Arjun and who Duryodhan, and now this Balbhadra had appeared to confuse her completely. Balbhadra!

Topi himself did not have a clear idea of who he was. The changes in him did not happen merely because of the political changes around him. His boyhood days too had contributed to shaping his particular kind of temperament. His childhood had been spent wearing clothes that were handed down to him from Munni Babu, and in submitting to the authority of Bhairav. He did not know that he had come to hate both his brothers. But Kallan? Where did Kallan come into all this? Although a part of the Students' Federation, he had not accepted the communist ideology in its totality. He disagreed with the Communist Party on several issues. Even when he had become a member of the Communist Party, he did not waver from his objections to those issues. He could never forgive the Party for taking sides with the British during the fight for Independence and for taking sides with the Muslim League on the issue of Pakistan. Where did Kallan come into all this? If he had not come to Benares, no one would have missed him. But he had come to Benares. Why? Somewhere deep within him was the hurt that Sakeena had refused to tie him a raakhi. It was because of this raakhi that he could not bring himself to tell Salima that he loved her. There were, before him, the precedents set by the couples Kishan Singh and Seema and Doctor Rayeez and Shakti. Yet he was afraid to tell Salima about his feelings for her.

Salima belonged to a Pathani family in Shahjahanpur. Golden complexion and big black eyes. When Salima had come to Aligarh, she was a staunch enemy of the Hindus. The first thing she learnt, when she arrived at Aligarh, was that Sakeena was having an affair with Topi. The moment she heard this, she began to dislike both Sakeena and Topi.

One day Topi presented a paper in a seminar held by the Hindi

Department. Salima had an argument with him. He had said that Hindi was a language of the Hindus and had then drawn the inference that a language spoken by the Hindus could not become a national language. 'Urdu is not the wife of any lecturer that she can be hooked. . . .' Topi's dark face went red.

This rocked the entire University. There was a stunned silence from Abdullah Hall right upto V.M. Hall.

This was that same day on which the story teller had begun this story when Topi had told Iffan that he'd like to fall in love with a Muslim girl. When Topi had said this he did not have Salima in mind even remotely. But when he thought about this later, he wasn't so sure.

One, two, three, four years passed. Salima debunked Topi all the time and on his part, Topi made fun of her all the time. . . . This went on for so long that their names started to be linked. Salima was called Topi's Salima and Topi began to be called Salima's Topi!

Please do not ask the story-teller why this Salima factor is being introduced so late in the story. This is the right moment to speak of Salima. I am not telling you a Salima-Topi love story, am I? But at this juncture I cannot proceed without talking about Salima. If that were possible I would not have mentioned Salima in this narrative at all. It is not the story-teller's business to pour out everything about the hero. A complete account of a life is very boring. A story-teller has to sieve out the boring parts.

Those who are not able to cut off the boring parts of their characters' lives cannot claim to be story-tellers. The art of story-telling lies more in concealing than in revealing. But this is possible only if the novelist knows everything about his characters. I know everything about Topi, that is why I have come so far and only then mentioned Salima. If I had brought in Salima right at the beginning then you would have assumed this to be another typical love story. You would have believed Salima to be the heroine of this story and then been happy or unhappy with the thought that by putting a Hindu boy and a Muslim girl into a romantic situation I was doing my bit for national integration. But I know that no integration takes place merely by providing a romantic situation. If this were possible then the conclusion of Premchand's *Maidan-e-Amal* would have been something totally different.

And so I'd like to tell you again that this is not Topi's love story but his biography. So I would request you to refrain from regarding Salima as the heroine of this story.

The fact was that talk of this Sakeena-Topi 'affair' was not limited to the Muslim University alone. Boys went home during vacations. If there were no vacation, boys wrote home asking for money. In a similar manner, news too travelled with these boys and their letters.

Munni Babu was the first to know that Topi was caught in an affair with Sakeena, a Muslim lecturer's wife. The first person Munni Babu mentioned this to was Bismillajaan. Please don't ask me what the point was in Munni Babu telling this to Bismillajaan. I too was quite amazed by this. But if in a market flourishing with thousands of Hindu prostitutes, Munni Babu chose a Muslim Bismillajaan, what am I to do?

'What's there to be scared of in this?' asked Bismillajaan. 'I too am a Muslim. Wasn't it only last year that my mother went to the Haj?'

'Your mother is not a prostitute.'

'Oh, you are so innocent.' Bismillajaan smiled. 'You don't even know who a prostitute is and who isn't. If we had not met in this market would you have ever known that I was a prostitute? Is it written on my forehead that I am a prostitute?'

'But . . .'

'Get your middle brother married. Even you were married off just to keep you away from Munnibai.'

'Wonder where she is now.'

'She's in some Khan Saheb's house in Ghazipur.'

'What!' Munni Babu was startled. 'Munnibai is in some Khan Saheb's house?'

'Yes.'

'But how can this be possible?'

'Why not?'

'Has she become a Muslim?'

'Is it necessary to become a Muslim to live in someone's house?'

Munni Babu poured out his anger over Munnibai's act of betrayal on Topi. He showed that letter to Doctor Saheb. Doctor Saheb remained silent. If Sakeena had not been someone's wife, he would have been disturbed. But after a few days when Bhairav, too, showed him a similar letter, he did get worried, and when Ramdulari told him the same thing one night, he was sunk in thought and decided to arrange for Topi's marriage even if it were not a decent enough bargain.

Balkrishna, a retired policeman, was unable to find a groom for his only daughter. He now found that groom. It was sheer coincidence that Topi had come to campaign for Kallan's elections at exactly the appropriate time.

'So, you've come to fight at the elections against your brothers?' asked Doctor Saheb.

'Yes, absolutely.'

'Aren't you ashamed of this?'

'If they are not ashamed to stand for the elections why should I be ashamed of canvassing for an election?'

'So, what is it—have you become a Communist?'

'Yes.'

'Who is Sakeena?'

Topi fell silent. He looked straight into his father's eyes.

'She is not my keep.'

'Then who is she?'

'She is the wife of a childhood friend of mine.'

'But . . .'

'Father, I . . .' he wanted to interrupt his father.

'I have finalized your marriage with Babu Balkrishna Rai's daughter,' Doctor Saheb cut him short.

'I will not consent to this marriage.'

Doctor Saheb was not used to this kind of speech in his house. Lost his temper.

'Get out of my house then.'

'A Hindu male becomes a legal heir from the very moment of his birth,' said Topi. 'But I would not wish to stay in a place where no one has even once bothered to find out what I want and where I have been accused of having an affair with my sister.'

Quietly, he left the room. No one even cared to think of where he would have been the whole day. But when he did not come home even at night, Ramdulari started getting anxious and then Doctor Saheb told her that he had asked Topi to leave home for good.

'What?' cried Ramdulari.

'Yes.'

'Where will he be . . .'

At that time Topi was in the waiting room writing a letter to Salima.

> . . . If you wish you may show this letter to Mumtaaz Aapa. And if she wishes to, she can have me rusticated. I would still like to say this to you today that I am so scared of you that I cannot keep you away from me. Can't we get married? You may say that you are a Muslim and that I am a Hindu . . . the children will be of a mixed breed. But isn't it possible for us to leave our children's concerns to them? My father has thrown me out of the home today. He too thinks that I have been having an affair with Sakeena. . . .

Topi read this letter over and over again several times. And then he tore it. He could not send it. He knew that such letters were written only in pulp fiction. In real life there was no possibility of writing these kinds of letters. But he felt unburdened after writing it. These matters had stuck to his gullet for a long time. He lay down and started thinking about Salima. He got up in the morning and had tea. And when this cup of tea wiped away the previous evening's exhaustion, he started thinking about what to do next. He couldn't possibly spend his whole life in a station, now could he?

He went straight to Kallan's house. Kallan cringed on seeing him.

'I'll stay here till the elections are over.'

'Here?' Kallan was shocked.

'Yes. My father has thrown me out of his home.'

Not Doctor Saheb. Not Munni Babu. Nor Bhairav. Not one of them had thought that Topi would so openly declare that he'd been thrown out of the house. . . .

The story-teller does not wish to bore you with an account of the speeches made by Topi. According to narrative tradition, heroes usually have to be great orators. Topi however was an awful speaker. So I'm going to omit the intricacies of the elections. How could you or I be interested in the victory or defeat of Kallan or Munni Babu? The elections were not a part of Topi's life. But being thrown out of the house was definitely an important event in his life. He wrote to Iffan:

> . . . I know now how happy your Baba Adam must have been on being thrown out of Paradise. Like my father's home, Paradise, too, must have been an excruciatingly boring place. Tell me Bhai, does it make any sense at all . . . if I wish to have an affair with your wife, do I first need to seek my father's *izaazat*/permission? Now I don't even have a home. Immediately make arrangements to see that I have a job, a home, and a homemaker. . . .

Iffan showed this letter to Sakeena.

'Although he's written izaazat instead of *ijaazat*, his letter is worth being considered seriously.'

'If I have no objections to having an affair with that blackie, why should that immature Doctor, that god-knows-what Narayan Shukla whatever, why should he have any objections?' asked Sakeena.

Iffan did not reply.

'Where is Topi Uncle's home, Baba?' asked Shabnam.

'From now on this is his home, child.'

'I can't feed that Hindu using my utensils,' said Sakeena with a sparkle of mischief. 'In any case, we needed a new tea-set.'

The matter ended there. Lying on the cot, eyes half-closed, Shabnam thought about her Uncle Topi. Iffan started reading the newspaper and Sakeena moved towards the kitchen.

XIV

❧

After coming back to Aligarh, the first news that reached Topi was about Salima's marriage. Shabnam gave him this news. When he came to Iffan's house directly from the station, there was no one at home except for Shabnam. Iffan had already left for the University and Sakeena was at the neighbour's.

'Topi Uncle, that was great fun,' said Shabnam.

'What?'

'Salima Aunty got married.'

'So where was the fun?'

'We were to go for the wedding. We missed the train,' and Shabnam started laughing.

Topi really had no right to feel sad. So he went towards the kitchen to make tea for himself. Shabnam followed him to the kitchen. Said: 'Uncle, I am feeling very bored.'

'What?' Topi was taken aback.

'Bored.'

'Ok, so you too are feeling bored.'

'What can I do? Everybody is getting bored. What does "bore" mean, Uncle?'

'Bore means bore.'

'Ammi has knitted a sweater for you.'

'What's it like?'

'Very beautiful. Uncle, aren't you a Hindu?'

'Why do you ask?'

'I had gone to Aunty Shaheeda's house yesterday. She was saying bad things about the Hindus to Aunty Mehmooda. So I told them, "Wah! Uncle Topi is also a Hindu. He is very nice." Both of them started laughing. Aunty Shaheeda said if the mother likes him why will the daughter not like him. Is Ammi very fond of you?'

'When did your Salima Aunty get married?'

'The day before.'

'When did you come?' Sakeena asked, entering the house.

'A few minutes ago. Was getting the latest from Shabnam.'

'So, that Doctor something-god-knows-what Shukla, he has completely disowned you, has he?'

'Not Doctor something-god-knows-what. He's Doctor Bhrugu Narayan Shukla of the Blue Oil.'

'Maybe.'

'Not maybe, but is,' said Topi. 'Just because I'm having an affair with you doesn't give you the right to make my father some god-knows-what.'

'Have you seen your face?' asked a sparkling Sakeena.

'I see it everyday.'

'You think I'd care to have an affair with a face like that?'

'Well, that's what the whole world is saying,' said Topi. 'Shabnam was telling me that Salima's got married?'

'Yes.'

'Just when I manage to fall in love with a Muslim girl, she goes and gets married off elsewhere.'

'Iffan has put in an application on your behalf.'

'To some girl's father?'

'Now I don't know if he is a girl's father,' said Sakeena, 'but he surely is the Registrar of this University.'

'For as long as you remain involved with me I cannot become a Lecturer here and Bhai cannot become a Reader! So I'm thinking if it's best to leave you.'

Sakeena fell into a shocked silence. Surely this was somebody else speaking?

'Don't be ridiculous.'

'I'm not being ridiculous. I am not bothered about you or myself or about Bhai. But Shabnam . . .'

'My daughter is not an ut or a but.'

'How long will you continue to hide the matter behind that façade of a smile? Why don't you tie me a raakhi?'

'Out of fear of what the mullahs here will say? Out of fear of the Jameelas and Anisaas and all the pure aapas here? Out of fear of all these cowardly Communists? I cannot tie raakhis on any Hindu. Your father Doctor something-god-knows-what of the Blue Oil has thrown you out of his house. Your brother has set aside a room for you here in this house. Stay here with us if you have the courage.'

Without waiting for Topi's reply, Sakeena went to her room. She wanted to cry, but she did not wish to break down in front of Topi or Shabnam. She was reminded of Ramesh whose letter still remained under her pillow. She started reading that letter again. The letter was in Urdu.

> Sukkan my sister! I am at the battlefront. I have no idea of what can happen. All around me is the eternal continuity of snow. I am very lonely here because I do not have your raakhi. Why have you changed so much Sukkan?. . .

The letter that had been written two months earlier had reached Sakeena two days ago, and on that same day the newspapers had carried a report on Colonel Ramesh's death while at the battlefront in Laddakh. On reading this piece of news, Sakeena had pulled out a box and started counting the raakhis that she had stored in it. That is what took her time and this is why they missed that train and could not attend Salima's wedding. Even Iffan did not know that she had a corpse of raakhis stashed away in a box. How could one leave a corpse at home and go for a wedding? And this Topi here has the gumption to ask me why I don't tie him a raakhi!

She took out fourteen raakhis from that box. She kissed each one of these and put them back into the box.

'Ay Bhabi!' Topi called out from the doorway.

'What's it?'

'What are you doing?'

'Thinking.'

'What are you thinking about?'

'I am wondering what it was that I could have seen in you to have kept my handsome moon-faced husband aside and have an affair with you.'

'The moon does not keep a beard.' Iffan said coming into the room. 'Yaar Topi, God knows what's happened to this woman since the last two days. She just goes on brooding.'

Sakeena did not want anyone to be a party to her grief. Her sorrow was such that it was difficult to explain. Everyone knew that she hated the Hindus. But no one knew that she had a box filled with fourteen raakhis. So which of these was true—her hatred which everyone knew of or those raakhis about which no one knew anything? It is not easy to differentiate between truth and falsehood. Perhaps Sakeena herself had no idea which of these two was a lie—her hatred or those raakhis.

'Irfan Habib is reading a paper today on *The Problems of National Integration*. It seems that Ikhtidaar Aalam Khan too is planning to say a few radically bold things,' Iffan told Topi.

'Khan is quite a veteran when it comes to making bold pronouncements,' said Topi.

'No integration takes place just because somebody is reading a paper on it,' said Sakeena. 'And even if that were to happen then, at best, people could become like Aale Ahmed Suroor or Ravindra Bhramar. No thanks, but I am happy with the upfront communal Hindus and Muslims.'

'Whenever you speak you have to say something unconventional,' said Topi.

'What's unconventional about this,' said a visibly annoyed Sakeena. 'Isn't it true that in order to make Khaleek Nizami a Professor as against Doctor Satish, a whole Muslim demonstration was engineered by Suroor Saheb? And isn't it also true that that same Khaleek Nizami was made Professor instead of Irfan Habib by the royal Communists? Only opportunists live in this University. In a few days Daan will become the Principal of the Women's College and you . . .' she turned towards Iffan, 'you will remain just a Lecturer. Majrooh Gorakhpuri will not find a place here and Khwaja Masood Ali Zouqi will get promoted. This country is for the likes of the Abrar Mustafas, Jazabis, Bhramars, and Nur-ul-Hasans. There is no place in this country for the Topis and the Iffans. Here, aapas who supply girls to the rich of this city will go around saying that I have an affair with Topi. And immediately after talking to the doctor about this they will, in the same breath, ask the doctor to abort another girl's child. I feel suffocated here. Just please take me away from here. . . .'

Topi and Iffan, stunned beyond words, gaped at her and she started sobbing loudly.

'That's why I keep imploring you to tie me that raakhi,' said Topi.

'Why should I tie you the raakhi?' Sakeena started screaming. A deep red anger burned in her big black eyes. 'I am not some aapa of this city. Whoever I tie a raakhi on, dies.'

'Who's died?' asked Iffan, a trifle worried.

'Nobody.'

'But . . .' began Topi.

'Nobody. A Hindu died.'

Sakeena wept as if she were insane. Iffan sat by her side and ran his fingers through her hair. Topi found his presence in the room redundant.

He could not touch Sakeena. He could not remain standing in the same place either. He started arranging the things that were lying on the dressing table. In a minute, this work was done. Sakeena was still crying.

Iffan was trying to calm her. Topi left them alone in the room and came out. Shabnam was lying on a cot and humming:

Jack and Jill
Went up the hill . . .

Topi did not wish to get embroiled in Jack's predicament, otherwise he would certainly have asked, the way he usually did, why Jack had to go up the hill in the first place. And Shabnam would have argued with him and they would have spent some time bantering like this.

'Who died?' It was almost as if Jack and Jill had asked this question. But Topi did not answer. He was very sad. He knew that Sakeena's hatred was only a façade. And that is why he was not hurt by her refusal to tie him a raakhi. He was hurt by the fact that she was weeping.

There was a crowd as usual at Bahadur's, the *paanwaala*. Apart from paan and beedi there seemed to be little else that people could afford to buy in the markets these days. The rest of the bazaar was dozing. Some boys were listening to Radio Ceylon at Tea Corner and Cozy Corner. The poster of *Tasveer Mahal* atop Lala's shop appeared forlorn. Ameen, as usual, was giving one of the boys a shave and was perhaps telling him how fond Saddar Ayub used to be of getting a shave done. And how the *nawaab*, Liaqat Ali Khan, did not have a shave for four days as he had gone to attend a wedding. How intoxicating those days were . . .

Everything was as it always used to be. The 'Riding Club' board in front of Doctor Nur-ul-Hasan's gate stood without a care in the world, taking in the smells of the dung of the horses meant to draw carriages. A cobbler, his head bent, was absent-mindedly repairing a worn-out shoe.

Everything was the same.

Some boys walked past Topi. They were talking about some girl. Then a group of boys started ragging a boy. That boy left the group, his head hung low.

Boys who were standing in front of Rahmat Café began to quarrel. Knives were pulled out. A Thai boy punched another's nose. The Proctoreal Bull did not interrogate the Thai boy but started taking down the name and address of the injured boy.

A truck crushed an insane girl running along the roadside and moved on without stopping. News came pouring from the All India Radio.

'What is this I hear—your father has thrown you out of his house?' Someone put his arm around Topi's shoulder.

'Yes.' Topi answered.

The person who asked this question was one of the senior bullies of this area.

'Introduce me, too—to your Sakeena—sometime.'

This was the first time that someone had so brazenly taken Sakeena's name in his presence. Topi shook with anger.

Boys who were walking by laughed out heartily. They had not heard what the bully had said. They were laughing at their private joke but Topi felt as if they were laughing at him. Then the whole bazaar started laughing. The poster and the riding-club board too started laughing.

'Shut up!' screamed Topi.

All laughter ceased immediately. Shamshad Market held its breath. Its face fell. Bahadur started making paan at a feverish speed. Sayyed Habeeb started speaking to a customer. Boys who were scattered here and there moved towards the tea-stall. Topi's lips felt parched. His heart started beating loudly against him.

'Shut up?' repeated the bully. He wondered how anyone could have the courage to see him straight in the eye and say 'shut up' to him. It was as if he had been openly humiliated. 'Shut up?' he murmured again.

Topi remained rooted to the spot.

Why doesn't he run away from here?—thought the bully.

There is really no point in getting into the details of what happened next. It is enough to know that when Topi regained his consciousness he found himself in a hospital. He had been stabbed by a knife several times and the Proctor could not find a single witness in the entire Shamshad Market. No one knew the culprit.

On the other side of the bridge, there were public demonstrations. Colleges remained closed. Shops remained shut. Rumours spread. People started hurrying homewards. . . .

There were riots. Then these riots spread towards the entire western part of UP—Merut, Shahjahanpur, Bareilly, Haathras, Khurja . . . dead bodies, dead bodies, dead bodies.

Dead body.

This is such a disgusting word! People who die in their own homes, in front of their own children, people who die their own deaths—even those bodies without souls are called dead bodies. And when men get killed by rioting mobs and die on the streets—even these bodies without souls are called just that—dead bodies. Language is such a beggar for words! There is such a dearth of right words. It is such a shameful thing that we do not have words that can differentiate between those who die at home and those who are murdered on the streets, despite the fact that at home only one person dies at a time while at the hands of mobs a whole generation gets eliminated, tradition gets murdered, culture dies, history dies.

The Bahuriya of Kabeer's Ram dies. Padmavati of Jhaansi dies.

Kutuban's Mrugaavati dies, Sur's Radha dies. Waaris' Heer dies. Tulsi's Ram dies. Anees' Hussain dies. No one sees this pile of dead bodies. We count dead bodies. Seven people were killed. Fourteen shops were looted. Ten houses were set on fire. As if all these—houses, shops, people—were mere words that have been pulled out of a dictionary and let loose to float around in space. . . .

Do you wonder why the story-teller has begun to pontificate? I beg forgiveness. You see I am not a leader. I have so much to say that there is no need for me to make a speech. These were things said by Topi. And he'd said it exactly like this—in these very words. He did not mispronounce any word while saying all this.

Newspapers, the radio, political leaders, and all Hindus and Muslims started focusing on the riots. All of them forgot that there was someone called Topi who was perhaps at this very moment languishing in hospital. Only Sakeena remembered him. She went to the hospital everyday. All patients, all the doctors, compounders, toilet-cleaners, rickshaw-drivers, Professors, Readers, their beloveds, and their wives looked at her with wonder. She continued to go to the hospital with her head held high. She would sit there with her head held high and she would return with her head held high.

Topi continued his speech on the same subject. A bored Shabnam would leave the room and take a walk in the lawns. When she returned to the room she would notice that the speech still hadn't ended.

'Why don't you understand that riots are a localized phenomenon? When there were riots in Jamshedpur, didn't you sleep well here in Aligarh?'

'Let's not talk about me,' said Sakeena. 'I don't sleep well even on normal days.'

'Why?'

'These snake-like raakhis writhe all over my body.'

'Raakhis?'

'Yes.'

'You must be mad,' said Topi, laughing.

'Don't laugh. The doctor has forbidden it.'

'What the hell! Now doctors even stop us from laughing, is it? In any case, where does one get the chance to laugh in this country?'

'You know, people like you, why do you make everything political?'

'Because we love to raise slogans and make speeches.'

'Iffan has shaved his beard.'

'What? When? And why? And when does he plan to let it grow again?'

'Don't know.'

Even Iffan did not know why he had let his beard grow and if he had once decided to have a beard, he did not know why he was against it now. When there were riots, he was very sad. One day Sakeena saw him come home with a shaving kit. Sakeena didn't ask him any questions.

'Arre, why don't you show me this clean-shaven person?'

'He's gone to Delhi.'

'Why?'

'He's resigned from college.'

'I never thought Bhai would be such a coward.' Topi started crying. 'Bhai has left me and has gone to Delhi without even telling me.'

'It has now become impossible to live here, Topi.'

'Why?'

'Why do you ask as if you don't know anything?'

'Then why do you keep coming here?'

'If you don't want me to, I won't come.' Saying this she left the room in such a hurry that Topi could not even utter a word. He hid his face in the pillow and wept like a child.

He was upset with Sakeena and Iffan and that's why when Sakeena came again in the evening to meet him, he didn't speak to her. Sakeena too did not speak to him.

'Why have you come now?' he asked angrily. 'You'd left in such a huff.'

'Am I your slave girl to take your permission and follow your word?' Sakeena burst out. 'What do you think of yourself? Who gave you the right to ask me these kinds of questions? Stick to your limits. Don't start getting ideas.'

Topi was stunned.

XV

❖

Iffan's resignation was accepted. The only person who refused to accept it was Topi.

'Listen Topi, the truth is that when you were in hospital I felt absolutely alone. We are incomplete without each other. I can put up with any amount of slanderous talk about Sakeena but neither I nor Sakeena can ever forget that these riots were caused because of Sakeena.'

'Let's not waste our time in such *fujool* talk.' Topi said this and looked at Iffan and Sakeena. He was dead sure that one of them would definitely correct him and say the word was *fuzool* (useless) and not fujool and then everything would be all right. But no one corrected him. He was deeply disturbed. It was as if life had been emptied of everything.

'Look Bhai, why do you forget that you are a Muslim? When bloody I am not able to get a job, how will you be able to find one?' Topi was getting worked up.

'Uncle, you are using bad words,' interrupted Shabnam.

'Who told you that bloody is a bad word?' Topi asked her.

'Look here Topi, there's no point in your getting angry,' said Iffan.

'Then what do you plan to do—go to Pakistan?'

'No. How can I go to Pakistan! Imam Hussain comes to India during Muharram. This year I'll meet him and ask him for how long those who speak the truth will continue to be punished.'

'For as long as man continues to tell lies,' answered Topi. 'I will be attending an interview tomorrow.'

'Where?'

'Sanatana Dharma Degree College, Bahraaich.'

'Why bother? You will not get the job,' said Sakeena.

'Don't you know I'm the hero of the riots? You may not have seen the

Hindi newspapers. My photographs are splashed all over the pages. My benevolent father has written to me saying that he has forgiven me and that there is this marriage proposal for me from a really illustrious family. My prospective father-in-law has promised me a plush job in Delhi, a very big car, a modest house, and a huge bank balance.'

'Get married immediately,' said Sakeena.

'Uncle Topi, I'll roam around in your car,' said Shabnam.

'Sure, sure. I'll have to get married just so that you can roam around.'

'So shall I go and tell this to Shobha and Phulli?'

'Tell them what?'

But Shabnam had already left to tell her friends that Uncle Topi was going to get a big car.

'Children become *khus*/happy with such small things.'

'*Khush*, not khus,' corrected Sakeena.

Topi felt alive again.

He wrote a letter to Doctor Saheb that very day telling him that he did not wish to have a car—big or small. He did not read this letter out to Sakeena or Iffan.

He quietly put the letter into the post box and took the train. He prepared for the interview throughout the journey. He revised the history of literature in his mind. He thought once more about the problems of literature. And when he entered the room where he was to be interviewed, he was fully prepared and also quite sure that he would not get this job.

'How is it that there are riots in your University almost every other day?' was the first question.

Literature!

History of literature!

Problems of literature!

'This University should be closed down,' said an expert.

Tradition of literature!

Continuity of culture!

'What do you think of Raskhaan—do you think he is a Hindu or a Muslim?' was a question asked.

'I consider Jaaysee too to be Hindu. And Ghalib and Meer too,' said Topi.

'How do you mean that?'

'Ghalib used to worship idols. All of Urdu literature believes in idol-worship. Meer had gone to the extent of applying a tilak on his forehead. Seated outside a temple, drawing from a hookah, he had given up Islam long ago.'

'This is a perspective that has never been thought of before.'

'It is not too late even now.'

That was the end of the interview. He returned to Aligarh.

'How did it go?' asked Sakeena.

'A country that has universities where people wonder whether Ghalib was a Sunni or a Shia and whether Raskhaan was a Hindu or a Muslim, I will not teach in such a country.'

'What will you do then?' asked Iffan.

'I'll write film songs. I'll polish shoes. I'll beg. I'll marry the only daughter of a rich man and live in peace. I can do any of these.'

'What are your chances?'

'There were two other candidates more qualified than me,' said Topi.

'And how many were called for the interview?' asked Iffan.

'Three.'

'Then you will get selected,' said Sakeena.

'*Yadi* (if) I get selected, I'll commit suicide.'

'Please spare me your "yadi padi", ok?' said Sakeena.

'I've got a job in Jammu,' said Iffan.

'What job?'

'To teach History.'

'Whose history—the one written by K.M. Munshi or the one by Khaleeq Nizami?'

'Why don't you mention Professor Habeeb's or Doctor Tarachand's names?'

'Who bothers about them these days?' Topi laughed. 'When do you have to leave?'

'Rightaway.'

'Bhai, get me also a job or a wife there.'

This matter was brushed aside as a funny remark. But Topi did seriously wonder about his life without Iffan, Sakeena, and Shabnam. He would be alone once again. Things were being packed. He packed the hold-all. He called for the rickshaw. He put the luggage into the compartment.

'You will write letters, won't you?' asked Sakeena.

'Uncle, bring that car and come to Jammu,' said Shabnam, and that saved him from having to reply to Sakeena.

The train left. He was left standing on the platform.

'The one who used to sell potions to heal the heart, she has moved shop.' A boy passed by humming this song. Topi turned to look at him. He turned and looked the other way.

The group that the boy belonged to started laughing and the sound of their laughter lashed at Topi like a whip.

XVI

Iffan left. Sakeena left. Shabnam left.

(Salima. . . . Well . . . she had already been married.)

Fate had nailed him to the cross of loneliness. And Aligarh had placed him on a sharp knife-edge of derisive laughter, snide remarks, oblique slights, and taunts and insinuations. Topi's blood boiled. Even those stabs from the bully's knife had not wounded him so much.

The identity of Maulana Balbhadra Narayan Topi Shukla disintegrated and fell into pieces. Three pieces had gone off to Jammu while a fourth remained in Aligarh. This fourth piece was surrounded by his own partly complete, partly incomplete, sinister shadow.

None of Topi's desires had ever got fulfilled. He had wished his mother could give him a cycle but what he got was Bhairav. He had wished that Sakeena would tie him a raakhi, but she went off to Jammu. He had wished that Salima would marry him, but she got her thesis written by him and then married some Sajid Khan. He'd wished for a job, but he was denied one either because he was a Hindu or because he was regarded as a Muslim. How many pieces can a man be split into! Topi had never taken the trouble to ponder over this issue. The truth is that only fictional heroes can think about such issues. Does life ever give one a chance to think? There was one thing however that Topi knew about himself for sure and that was that he could never make compromises. And honestly, this was the only reason why Topi did not leave Aligarh despite the departure of Iffan, Sakeena, and Shabnam. This decision to stay back turned out to be the most significant one of his life. Topi did not even know that he had taken a very significant decision. Topi was never to know the import of this decision. But the story-teller learnt a few days later that this decision was a climax in Topi's life. And so the story-teller seeks your permission to allow him to pause here for a moment, for the time has now come to answer all those questions that have been plaguing your mind. I am not a novelist who can claim that the story is mine and will therefore choose to disclose what I please and conceal whatever I wish to. I am not saying that the writer of a novel can be whimsical. He, too, can be questioned and he, too, is answerable—but both the kinds of questions asked and the kinds of answers that may be given are different. There is this difference between a biography and a novel. A biographer cannot add anything from his side to the story. He cannot even change the sequence of events. But a novelist can create his own sequences of events according to his will. And he says everything on his own behalf. If I were writing a novel and if Topi were the hero of that novel then I would not have allowed him to say 'fir' instead of 'phir'. But Topi is not my creation. He was created by Doctor Bhrugu Narayan Shukla of the Blue Oil and Ramdulaari. And he used to say 'fir' instead of 'phir'. If I had corrected his speech, this would have been disloyal to his life's story. That is why writing a biography is far more demanding than writing a novel.

Topi is not the hero of a romance narrative. He could not have ever been the hero of a romantic story. It is only with great difficulty that he has managed to be the hero of his own biography. He belongs to that group of people who cannot figure as the central character even if the story is about their own lives. Topi, like all people of this era, was an incomplete individual. He could never become complete without the help of another individual. That is why I have tried to put all his disparate pieces together. When he was in Benares, he was incomplete without Munni Babu and Bhairav—one could also include Iffan here. And when he came to Aligarh, he did not come with his personality complete. Munni Babu and Bhairav remained behind in Benares and Iffan had been separated from him even earlier.

In Aligarh, he had remained floating like an unanchored kite until he met Iffan. And then Iffan, Sakeena, and Shabnam together made him whole. But these three, too, were in themselves incomplete. Iffan was incomplete without his Daadi, his Abbu, and his Baaji. That is why I had to include them in this narrative. Sakeena was incomplete without her father Sayyed Aabid Raza, Mahesh, and Ramesh. So I had to talk about them. Shabnam has to be understood in connection with Sister Alema. In order to understand Munni Babu one has to be familiar with Munnibai and Bismillajaan, and in order to understand Bhairav, one has to see Kallan for whose sake Topi went to Benares. I am saying all these things so that you will not wonder why so much space has been given to irrelevant people or 'supporting characters' when the central story actually belongs to Topi.

Incompleteness and loneliness are perhaps the fate of the Topis of this era. Had he been born a thousand or fifteen hundred years earlier, his story would have been different. He would, by now, have been killed while fighting somebody else's battle. Then perhaps I would not have included so many people in the story. A problem that worries me is that this is not a biography of a great man. This is the biography of a small man. My hero is not even a Raj Kapoor or a Dilip Kumar. That is why his incompleteness bothers him. That is why after Iffan, Sakeena, and Shabnam left he remained a solitary lonely figure. An empty house. A house that was empty but could not be given on rent.

After leaving the station he realized that he had nowhere to go. Well, there still was that house in which Iffan had lived till a few hours ago. He could continue to stay in that rented apartment for another twenty days. Iffan had paid the entire month's rent. The very thought of that house, however, filled him with dread.

An auto-rickshaw driver solved his problem. The auto belonged to Shamshad Market Square. The driver recognized Topi. He started the rickshaw as soon as he saw Topi. 'Come in miyaan,' he said, patting the seat of his rickshaw.

Topi had spent his entire life taking orders from others, so he quietly got into the auto. The rickshaw moved forward. The driver did not even ask him where he wished to go. Not just the auto-driver, everybody in the University knew where he usually went.

The rickshaw stopped in front of the house where Iffan used to live, where Topi used to quarrel with Sakeena, where Shabnam used to teach him English.

He found it very strange taking a bunch of keys from his pocket and opening the lock, for this house had always stood open to him.

He entered the house.

The house was the same. The rooms were the same. The colours on the walls were the same. The plants in the pots kept in the garden were the same. Shabnam's *juhi* plant was heavy with buds. The breeze continued to peep into the rooms, to sway in the terrace, to smile in the garden, to tickle the plants—in the same way. The poor plants seemed to be rolling in laughter.

He peeped into Iffan's room. There were no books in the built-in shelves. The place where Iffan's chair used to be, now stood vacant. The place where the pedestal lamp used to be—that remained unchanged. Iffan had left that lamp for Topi.

An eerie feeling pushed Topi out of that room.

There was silence in Sakeena's room. He sat on the window-sill and looked at the bare floor where earlier there used to be three beds. A smouldering stub of Charminar lay in a corner of the room—almost ready to burn out completely. He bent to pick up the stub. Then he dropped it half-heartedly and left the room.

He did not feel comfortable at home. He was afraid that if he stayed here a moment longer, he would start crying. So he locked the house and wandered aimlessly towards Shamshad Market.

It was a cold December night. Like the characters in detective films and stories, people had pulled up their overcoat collars and were walking along rapidly. There was a crowd as usual at Bahadur's shop. In the shop facing this, Sayyed Habeeb with his dramatic beard was talking in his usual (meaning high-pitched) voice.

'Alone now, partner?' came a voice from Cozy Corner and some boys started laughing. Topi knew that this remark was addressed to him. But Sakeena had already left for Jammu with Shabnam and Iffan. So what was the point in turning around? He moved on ahead. Aaftaab Manzil to his left and the swimming pool to his right were plunged in darkness. Some light filtered out of the rooms of Sahab Baug but Topi walked on, mindless of the light trickling out.

> It is for this reason alone they tell you not to fall in love.
> See, you are left alone Yussuf, as a good-for-nothing.

Some boy from a group recited this couplet loudly. This voice lashed at Topi and left its indelible mark on his soul. Obviously, there was nothing that Topi could say. He had stayed behind in Aligarh even though Iffan had insisted that he leave. Now he was paying the price for staying back.

He moved towards Azaad Cafeteria. He knew that he'd be able see a few familiar faces there.

Right in front stood Wajid Ali Khan, the owner of this canteen. Managing his obese body, he was perhaps trying to explain some literary problem to Jazabi. On seeing Topi, Wajid Khan smiled. . . .

XVII

I seek your permission to allow me to introduce a new character
towards the fag end of this story. I know this is against the rules of
story-telling. But these were rules made very long ago. This is the
right moment in which to meet Wajid Khan. The point is that even if
Wajid Khan's own life were to be chronicled, he would appear at its very
end! Then how could I have introduced him at the very beginning while
we are engaged in Topi's life?

No one who saw Wajid Khan could ever take him for a poet. He was,
however, quite a foppish poet. The literary world knew him as Javed
Kamaal. He used the name Wajid Khan to sell tea at the University
canteen! The story-teller has always wondered about his real identity—is
he really Wajid Khan or Javed Kamaal? He worshipped paan, and loved
words and things of beauty. He had perforce to listen to his own voice
for, in our world, no one listens to those who have no agents to promote
them. He talked continuously for he feared that if he kept quiet for some
length of time he, too, might forget that he had a voice. His family
insisted that he was Wajid Khan and he insisted that he was Javed Kamaal.
And that this Wajid Khan had clung to him like a ghost. In order to get rid
of this ghost, he was willing to spend hours talking about the problems of
literature even with such ordinary, unintelligent, and lowly poets as
Jazabi. He would treat his friends and acquaintances to free tea as well. He
was a normal person but because he was surrounded by bald angels, he
appeared to be abnormal.

You must be wondering why I have abandoned Topi's story and have
begun talking about Wajid. So I would like to tell you rightaway that
Wajid too is an inseparable part of Topi's story. One act of this drama was
played on Wajid's stage. We are now close to the point where the breeze

will turn a page of Topi's story and lay bare that page to us. So I consider it important to show you the stage where the play was enacted. Wajid had a big role to play in bringing Topi and Salima together.

When Topi was alone in Aligarh, he used to spend a lot of time with Wajid. This should give you an inkling of how important Wajid is. And this is why I bring Wajid into the picture. . . .

Wajid could have become a great body-builder. He became a poet instead. Otherwise, he too could, like Dara Singh, have become a film star. Girls found his bright honey-coloured eyes fascinating and he was not used to working in the dark. So if one were to think of how he spent his life—for life continues to move—then it was really spent in helping friends. He would wait for someone to fall in love and then he would take over from there. He could heap so much advice on the one who was in love that the fellow would give up in despair or get depressed and fall in love with another girl!

I have forgotten to tell you the most important thing about Wajid. He was Iffan's friend. Both did their B.A. together. Then Iffan moved on to major in History and he majored in Urdu. Iffan cleared his M.A. with a first class and became a Lecturer while Wajid started selling tea. Well, Wajid sold shoes, too, for some time. Friends, poets, and novelists however, bought so many pairs of shoes on credit that he went out of business. If God so willed, his canteen too would face a similar fate!

Iffan had introduced Wajid to Topi. When Wajid learnt that Topi was Iffan's childhood friend, he started believing that Topi was his childhood friend too! Really, this is just the kind of person Wajid is.

There was nothing in common between him and Topi. He worshipped beauty and Topi was a classic example of the ugly. He loved music and Topi belonged to a family that had never been able to carry a tune. He hated Hindi and Topi was like an election symbol for Hindi. He loved to eat paan and Topi was like an advertisement for Binaca toothpaste. The two had just one meeting ground. He loved to talk and Topi was used to listening. He would speak for hours and Topi would listen to him talk for hours.

One day, Jazabi was inflicting a story on Wajid. This bald angel was telling him a story about a friend's middle-aged maid-servant who had fallen in love with him and had offered him a bottle of Brylcream to use on his bald pate. While recounting this story, a lewd spark lit up Jazabi's eyes; he displayed his dirty teeth and started laughing. Just like a person who, plagued by an itch for a long time, scratches on the itchy patch and starts to enjoy the sound made by the scratching, Jazabi too laughed with a similar 'khi-khi' scratchy sound. Jazabi's soul, in fact, had been attacked by this itchy virus for a long time! While listening to this story Wajid was actually trying to hide a yawn behind a smile.

'Your *saayari* (poetry) is better than these things you talk of,' said Topi. 'Why did you leave your saayari?' asked Topi deliberately mispronouncing *shaayari*.

Jazabi's laughter stopped abruptly.

'You are a student and you dare to talk like this?' said Jazabi, raising his voice in anger.

'Arre Sir, if a teacher can talk so shamelessly why should I feel ashamed to say anything?' asked Topi.

'Shut up, you illiterate.' Wajid's eyes flashed.

'Wajid Bhai, you too get bored by this talk but you don't have the courage to say it. You must be quite pleased in your heart of hearts that I have spoken your mind. Do you think I was interested in listening to all that rubbish about that middle-aged maid servant?'

Jazabi Saheb got angry and left in a huff. After he'd left, Wajid looked at Topi and smiled.

'You are really bloody troublesome, I must say . . .'

'Honestly, I fear that some day while teaching some Ghalib-Walib this man might start talking of some maid's story.' This time Topi pronounced the word *shuru*, meaning start, correctly.

'*Shabaash*!' said Wajid, patting him on his back. 'You've pronounced the word shuru absolutely correctly!'

There was a burst of loud laughter and exactly at this moment Salima entered the canteen with a Lecturer. Topi was the first to see her enter.

'Bhai, do something about this silly girl,' said Topi. 'She has made my life miserable (*haraam*).'

'Shut up you Hindu!' said K.P. 'What do you have to do with haraam and *halaal* (ethical and unethical)?'

Topi was quite taken aback for K.P. himself was a Hindu.

'One slip of a girl has made life haraam for you and you go around whining about it. Shame on you.'

'Plant your steps cautiously, child!' said Wajid. 'She's a Pathani from Shahjahanpur. She'll pound you like paddy and spread you out in the open courtyard to dry.'

'Topi, this alone should be reason enough for you to fall for her,' said K.P.

'The hell, if you try to entice any Muslim girl with so much as even throwing an oblique glance, I'll chop your legs and throw them away,' said Wajid.

'No, Bhai,' said Topi in all earnestness, 'no, I'll not throw an oblique glance, but I can look straight at them, can't I?'

'Straight? Not even if you try a million times,' said Wajid testily. 'You are like a dog's tail—can never remain straight.'

'Bhai, you are very communal,' said Topi, smiling.

Wajid pounced on this word 'communal'. He started using abusive terms and when he ran out of expletives, he came back to the moot issue. ' I cannot grant a Kaalicharan (blackie) like you permission to fall in love with such a beautiful girl. Have you ever seen your face? You are like an ad for Kiwi and . . .' he went on to explain this simile.

'Bhai, is this face of mine eligible to fall for a lentil face?' asked Topi, with all-assumed innocence.

Wajid broke into a raucous laughter. The canteen was hushed into silence. Salima turned to see where the sound of the laughter had come from.

'This place is now no longer fit for decent people,' said Salima's escort.

Boys sitting at a corner table started tapping a glass with a spoon asking for their bill so that they could pay up. This was when Salima's escort realized that he had no money with him. Coincidentally, Salima too did not have money with her. Her escort was deeply embarrassed. He started to perspire. Salima took a decisive step towards Wajid.

'Wajid Bhai!' She came close to him and said, 'I received Fakhroo Bhai's letter yesterday. He sends you his regards.'

Salima had passed on her cousin brother Fakhroo's greetings to Wajid after some four and a half years. When she was to come to Aligarh for a B.A. course, Fakhroo had sent a letter from Karachi for Wajid through her. Salima had not bothered to pass on that letter to him. Fakhroo would enquire about Wajid in each one of his letters and Salima would write back to him saying that Wajid says this and Wajid says that and so on. When the matter of this bill cropped up, she had no alternative but to go and meet Wajid.

'Please sit down, please sit,' said Wajid. Topi moved over to one side. Salima sat next to him. The Lecturer sat facing them. 'Some tea or something?'

'No, thanks, we've just had some.'

'Have you paid?'

'Not yet. It's . . .'

'What is Fakhroo doing these days?' A waiter arrived and placed the bill in front of the escort. Wajid quickly picked up the bill and swore at the waiter forgetting that there was a lady seated in front of him.

'But Wajid Sahab, you can't . . .'

'Listen Mister, she's come here with news of Fakhroo after four and a half years,' said Wajid. 'Now get moving from here,' he dismissed the waiter angrily. The waiter left with a smile. 'This Fakhroo, too, used to be a strange fellow, Topi,' said Wajid. 'When he was here he claimed to be an atheist. After going there he's busy proving the existence of Allah miyaan. I am told that he earns a salary of some three to four thousand rupees.'

'There's a great deal of money that can be made these days by professing faith in Allah miyaan, Bhai,' said Topi.

'I'm sure you've met him?' Wajid asked Salima indicating towards Topi. 'He is the Muslim League Hindu here.'

Salima smiled.

'Ok Bhai, I'll leave now,' said K.P. getting up to go.

They ignored him. He left. Wajid started talking about Fakhroo. Salima was forced to listen to him. Her escort kept looking at his watch. He was waiting for Wajid Khan to complete his story so that he could take leave. But he did not know Wajid Khan too well. The story-teller has known Wajid Khan for some seventeen or eighteen years. To date, Wajid Khan has never been able to finish narrating any episode that he has started on. I have been hearing the same episode, again and again, for the last seventeen or eighteen years. I remember each one of them by heart. The episode that has remained inconclusive for these seventeen or eighteen years, continues to hang in the air even today. It is Wajid's style to take a topic to its climactic peak and pull another episode out of it from there. That is why when we get talking with Wajid we usually pull our watches off our wrists and stow them in our pockets. The poor Lecturer! How was he to know of this! It was time for him to take his class. He could not lose his job in his eagerness to entice Salima, now could he? That is why he got up while Wajid was still speaking:

'Excuse me,' he said, 'I have to go to class.'

'And Fakhroo burst out laughing. I must tell you this funny thing . . .' Wajid continued to speak to Salima, unmindful of the interruption. Now what could Salima do? She forced a smile. The escort cursed Wajid Khan in his heart of hearts and left the place. After he left, Wajid Khan shifted his bulk to change his posture. Taking out a small packet from his pocket, he ate a paan. 'Look here lady, you are Fakhroo's sister. So take this piece of information for what it is worth. The man you came in with is a crook. He speaks badly of you behind your back. He is a rogue. Does not take chances. Has multiple affairs going . . .'

'Wajid Bhai, what are you saying?' said Salima.

They chatted about other things for some time. And Salima did not even realize that she was conversing with Topi. When Salima left, Wajid had his third paan.

'Bhai, when that poor fellow was leaving you took absolutely no notice of him.'

'Are you crazy? You idiot.' Wajid spoke in the tone of someone who's seen it all. 'If I had paid attention to him, Salima too would have left with him.'

'So do I have your permission to fall in love with her?' Topi asked, looking straight at him.

'Topi. Listen to this.' Wajid became serious. 'Fakhroo had written to me about her. When she was new here. Fakhroo was not a friend of mine. Only an acquaintance. This girl is probably his fiancée. So go ahead and flirt with her if you wish but don't drag me into it.'

This was during the time when Salima had left the hostel and had moved over to live in her Chacha's house in Ameer Nishan. Her Chacha, apart from being her Chacha, was also a retired policeman.

Around the same time, a gentleman, fresh from Hyderabad or Secunderabad, arrived here to teach Psychology. His name was Dr Wahid Anjum. He used to think that the prefix 'doctor' was an integral part of his name, so I too am using his full name. He seemed incomplete without the tag of 'doctor'. Was a famous Urdu poet. Well, Aligarh is a dense jungle of poets. He was welcomed with open arms. This welcome sent him into raptures. As a result he started behaving as if he were on back-slapping terms with stalwarts like 'Majnoon' Gorakhpuri. He started believing that he was 'the poet' after Ghalib. And well . . . who the hell was Ghalib anyway!'

As a consequence, he continued to become friends and then quarrel with people like Khalil-ur-Rehmaan of Aazamgarh and Kaazi Abdus Sattaar of Sitapur.

Wahid Anjum is a part of this story because of Salima. Suddenly, one day, without any prior thought, he fell head over heels for Salima. But she was in the Hindi section and he was in Psychology—how could they meet? The poor fellow continued to pine for her. And all the while she was gradually getting closer and closer to Topi.

It wasn't a feather in Topi's cap—befriending Salima. I have already told you that Salima used to hate Topi. So one day she told Wajid: 'Wajid Bhai, may I ask you something?'

'Sure.' Wajid adjusted the paan in his mouth with great difficulty.

'How do you tolerate a leech like Topi?'

Wajid got up and placing his mouth close to the window bars, spat out the paan. One last drop of betel juice fell on his sherwani. Wiping it with a kerchief, he came back to where Salima was.

'What do you mean?'

'Well . . . people say that he's having an affair with Zargaam Saheb's wife?'

'Do you know the number of men people say you are having an affair with?' Salima's eyes opened wide in disbelief. She knew that there was a long list of men who were interested in her. But she did not know that people had linked her with so many of them. 'For instance, you are involved with that dark butterfly of the Hindi Department.'

'I had reported him to Mr Sharma.' Sparks of fire flew from Salima's eyes. 'He used to call me home. He apologized to me in Mr Sharma's presence and now he calls me Salima *behen*.'

'I'm sure he calls you that,' said Wajid a trifle disinterestedly. 'Another girl too had reported against him before you. So where was I—yes, about the number of people you are allegedly involved with. You may not know this but you are also supposed to be involved with that stupid leech with whom you had come here the other day. You are also supposed to be involved with Zaidi from your Department. And you are also involved with me!' Wajid thrust two stuffed and folded paan into his mouth angrily. Salima's face fell. 'Young lady, this is a very small place. And quite a few small-minded people too live here . . .'

Their conversation had only reached this far when Topi joined them: 'Hello Bhai!' He smiled, joining them at their table.

'She was asking me how I could put with a person like you considering that you are having an affair with Sakeena.'

Topi's dark face reddened. Salima was shocked. In his fury, Wajid chewed his paan vigorously.

'Bhai,' Topi told Wajid, 'look, I am going to try and tell what I think is right.' He stood up and told Salima, 'One can be grateful to God that I am not involved with you.' Having said this, he hastily turned away and left the canteen.

'Why did you tell him all this Wajid Bhai?'

Wajid's mood was already quite spoiled. Without waiting to give her a reply, he went to the counter to settle the bills. On seeing Iffan enter, Salima went cold. She greeted him. There was no vacant table in the canteen. He stood where he was.

'Some tea, Sir?' asked Salima.

'Don't call me sir-"vir" please,' said Iffan, joining her. 'You are Fakhroo Bhai's sister and he used to be my friend. Wajid knows this that whenever there were plans to beat up the S.F. boys, Fakhroo Bhai would tell me,

'Bhai please don't attend the meeting today'. But I would still go. And his hands would lose their punch while beating me. Once, as it happened, I had Gulrez Khan in my hold. Fakhroo shouted from where he was beating up Kanwar Amanat that Khan Saheb was a friend, so take care.' Iffan burst out laughing and turned towards Wajid, 'Yaar Wajid, do you have any news of Gulrez Khan?'

Wajid left the counter and came back to this table. He was still in a foul mood. As soon as he came to the table, he told Salima, 'Ask him how he puts up with Topi.'

Iffan laughed heartily. 'Oh dear! So you too have the same problem?' Then in a serious tone he said, 'Young lady, this University of ours is a strange place.' The waiter arrived, so Iffan told Salima, 'Well . . . there is no point talking about these kinds of things. What will you have to drink?'

'Wajid Bhai just got me some tea.'

'So now let Iffan Bhai buy you tea.' He turned towards the waiter. 'Coffee for Wajid Khan and tea for the two of us, quickly. I have to leave in fifteen minutes.' The waiter left. He started talking to Salima again. 'Sakeena always enquires about you. You haven't come home for over a year or a year-and-a-half. If you are not too busy why don't you come home with me now? I am going home. And yes, Wajid, I came here to remind you that it's Shabnam's birthday today. And if this year too you don't come you'll be done for.'

The waiter served tea. Salima started pouring it into the cups. She felt rather strange having tea with Iffan and although Topi was not there she continued to feel embarrassed in her heart of hearts.

She got up to leave along with Iffan.

Sakeena was thrilled to see her and seeing her so openly joyful, Salima felt so ashamed that she started weeping like a child. Sakeena got scared.

'What is the matter? You must tell me.'

'Nothing Bhabi.'

'You are a grown-up girl and yet you cry?' said Shabnam. Salima hugged her and laughed. Just then, they heard Topi's voice at the entrance.

'Is there anyone who will give Topi a cup of tea?' His eyes fell on Salima. Immediately he fell silent.

Iffan could sense the tension in the air, so he quickly began with: 'What happened at that anti-Urdu meeting?'

'A rejulation was passed,' said Topi.

'Arre, if you are against Urdu then speak *Urdu* wrongly, how has poor English harmed you?'

'Meet this man, Salima!' said Sakeena. 'He is some God-knows-what-Narayan-Shukla, alias Topi. Son of some God-knows-what-Narayan of

the Blue Oil. And more importantly, he is in love with me and I am
having an affair with him.'

'She knows this,' said Topi.

Salima was so embarrassed she wished the earth would swallow her.

'Yaar, Bhabi, why do you flaunt your love affair so brazenly?'

'What do you mean—using this "yaar vaar" like road-side loafers? If
you are a lover then you must sing a song. The way the heroes sing for
these two-bit heroines. Ay Topi, come on, let's have a song from you.'

Salima was a changed person when she left this house that evening. She
thought about Topi all the way home. And even as she fell asleep that
night, she continued to think about Topi.

Her Chaachi was angry with her son for he went to see films without
informing her. He would return at one or one thirty and ruin everybody's
sleep.

'You go to sleep Chaachi!' said Salima. 'I'll keep awake.'

'How long can you keep awake child?' said her Chaachi, who went off
to sleep soon after while Salima kept awake.

Deep into the night, there was a knock at the door. Salima opened the
latch. Instead of her brother, Doctor Wahid Anjum stood at her door.

It had so happened that Doctor Wahid Anjum had gone to the National
to have a shot of rum along with two scholars from the Urdu Department.
These two were great poets. All three got so hopelessly tipsy that they
began to think that they were the world's best poets. The matter reached
a point where they started abusing one another. The two Urdu poets went
off leaving the Psychology poet alone. Doctor Anjum felt greatly relieved
by this. He started reading out his poems to a waiter. That poor fellow got
bored for he was quite certain that Doctor Saheb would not tip him. Also
the fact that Doctor Saheb was using a very complicated Urdu.

'Police!' he said, instead of the expected "wah-wah". Doctor Saheb was
not so drunk as not to know what would happen if a policeman was
around.

The silence on Station Road floated like a cool breeze. Doctor Saheb's
spirits soared. And whenever he was in high spirits, he would automatically think of Salima. His inebriated state gave him courage. That is why
he forgot his own house where his simple wife was waiting for him. He
knocked on Salima's door.

Salima had barely opened the door when he opened his arms and
started: 'I'll make you immortal in my poems. You are the princess of my
dreams . . .'

Had Salima not screamed when he flung wide his arms, he would
perhaps have made a very long speech. But she did scream. The retired

policeman heard her and he did just what any retired policeman, or for that matter, any self-respecting person would have done. Meaning that he first gave Doctor Saheb some five to ten blows. Doctor Saheb was a weak man; he crumbled. His glasses broke and fell off his face.

'What happened, child?' the policeman asked Salima.

'He was . . .' and Salima stopped.

That Salima could not complete her sentence was evidence enough for Chaacha. He began to beat the poet again. Poor Doctor Wahid Anjum! His intoxication was completely wiped out.

Chaacha hauled him forward by his collar and told him, 'Let's go to the Police station.'

Doctor Saheb quivered on hearing the words 'police station'.

'I am a Lecturer in the University,' he said with abject supplication. 'I'll lose my job.'

Job!

This is such a frightening and lowly word. Wahid Anjum did not think of his reputation, maybe because there is nothing called reputation these days. Jobs have taken the place of reputation now.

How could Chaacha believe that a teacher, belonging to a University that was caught between live and dead traditions, could do such a thing? Doctor Saheb quickly remembered that one of his students lived close by. The student was woken up. He gave evidence. What could the Chaacha do now? He kicked Doctor Saheb on his back and threw him out of the compound.

He had, however, been a police officer. It suddenly struck him that Doctor Saheb could file a report and so, as a cautionary measure, he went to the police station at Civil Lines to file his report. (This matter was hushed up by the time it was morning. But in the records of the Civil Lines police station you will still find that report.)

You must be wondering why this incident is being described in so much detail. As I have told you earlier, I am not writing a thriller. So I will tell you the importance of this incident rightaway. It was important to relate this event because this fiancée of Fakhroo's who carried on an affair (carried on, not was in love) with Topi for two years, eventually married this very Doctor Wahid Anjum. The story-teller believes that this matter cannot be easily understood, and also believes that just because this matter cannot be understood he is not obliged to get Salima married off to Fakhroo or Topi. If I were building castles in the air, I would have got Salima married off to Topi in the name of national integration. But I am neither building castles in the air nor am I running this national integration scheme. I am merely introducing you to Topi, to his close circles, to his environment. I am not convinced about the need to hide things in order to build the element of suspense. That is why I have already told you that Salima did not marry Topi. And I am telling you now that she married Doctor Wahid Anjum. This marriage however did not happen easily. Doctor Saheb had to go to Pakistan in order to marry Salima. After going there, he had to say that Kashmir belonged to Pakistan and that the figures shown in the Indian census lied when it said that the Indian Muslim population was close to five crores. All the Indian Muslims had been killed in riots. He was the lone Muslim left alive and that he had just about managed to escape to Pakistan. To the query as to why news about riots still continued to come from India, he replied that India occasionally circulated this kind of news so that the world would not come to know that now there were no Muslims at all in India. The outcome of all this was that Doctor Saheb became a part of the Pakistani delegation to represent the Kashmiri cause and reached the Assembly Hall of the UNO. When he returned, he was made the Vice-Chancellor of a new University. Obviously Fakhroo did not stand a chance at all now! And here in Aligarh, Salima had got her thesis written by Topi and now there was nothing that could impede her wedding with Doctor Saheb. A quick engagement was followed by an equally quick wedding.

This episode that I just mentioned to you about the Doctor being beaten up is important because that led to an intense friendship between Salima and Topi.

What happened was that the very next day news spread round the University that Doctor Saheb had been beaten up the previous night. The people largely responsible for spreading this news were those who had spent that night getting drunk with Doctor Saheb.

The strange thing that happened too was that Doctor Saheb, in the wake of the beatings, really fell in love with Salima. Started making frequent visits to the Hindi Department. But Salima wanted to complete her Ph.D. And Wahid Anjum's salary in those days was not too decent.

The misunderstanding with Topi, too, had been cleared in Salima's heart. So she used to be seen moving around with Topi. There was quite a stir all around. Topi and Salima's names began to appear together in the local scandal reports. One rag went to the extent of publishing that Topi and Salima were secretly married. (This piece of news is absolutely unfounded, for had this been true, Topi would not have written that letter to Salima in the waiting room of Benares station—the letter that he wrote and then later tore up.)

From here onwards we have two camps. One that believed that Salima was a very brave girl who despite all the talk about her continued to be seen with Topi. (The storyteller belonged to this camp). The other camp believed that she was merely interested in her thesis. Iffan belonged to this other camp. This was the reason why when Topi returned from Benares, Iffan or Sakeena did not tell him a word about Salima's marriage.

Whatever be the truth, poor Topi's involvement was in vain.

'Bhai, she is very sincere.'

'Yes,' said Iffan, lighting his Charminaar and nodding his head, 'she is very sincere to herself.'

'You are jealous.' Topi was annoyed.

'Ay, be careful—don't you dare say such things about my husband!' flared Sakeena.

Shabnam laughed out loudly.

'I am not changing my opinion just because it annoys you,' said Iffan.

'You are jealous because I am having an affair with a Muslim girl. Beneath your skin, all you Muslims are Pakistanis.'

'Yes,' nodded Iffan. 'You are right upto a point. Pakistan is the name of an unnamed fear. And every Muslim is scared. What is this a fear of, Balbhadra? And why is there this fear? Why are you suspicious of me? And why am I scared of you . . .'

'Here, take care of your husband.' Topi said to Sakeena, 'He's got into his usual fit.'

'No, Balbhadra, seriously,' said Iffan. 'These two words, like dacoits, have made such a big nation their hostage. And these two dacoits are now demanding ransom.'

Fear!

Suspicion!

Muslim!

Hindu!

Black-White!

There was silence in the house. Iffan, along with Sakeena, Shabnam, and Topi was drowned in the poisonous sea of the question that he had raised. It was as if darkness had crawled in and covered the courtyard and the large expanse of sky spread above the open courtyard while a dimmed moon was resting its chin on top of a neem tree.

'But weren't we talking about Salima?' Topi's voice resounded in the darkness.

'Salima too is a blossoming fruit of that same tree of fear and suspicion. Pay serious attention to what I say Balbhadra, this same fear will consume her one day. Write her thesis for her quietly. Once she becomes Doctor Salima, she'll forget you.'

'But . . .'

'But what?' Iffan cut him short. 'But only this that she might even end up marrying Doctor Wahid Anjum but she will not marry you.'

'Why?' asked Topi. 'Is it because I am a Hindu?'

'No. Kishan Singh is also a Hindu,' said Iffan.

'Then what could the reason/*kaarun* be?'

'Where is the need to utter such a long and deep "unn"? Couldn't you have just said "kaarun"?' asked Iffan.

'Yaar, Bhai, I am talking about my love story and you are engrossed in your language improvement programme. You Urdu people are jealous of us Hindi people.'

'Not jealous, we fear you,' said Iffan.

Oh dear, not that same word again!

Fear!

Is there no possibility of getting rid of this fear? I am that Hindi and I am that Urdu. So does it mean that I fear myself too? One of my forms does not know one script. So he fears that other script. The war of languages, actually, is a war of monetary gain and loss. The issue at heart is not language. The issue is employment.

Employment.

This word too confronts us at all kinds of junctures. The form that knows a particular script feels safe. That which does not know a particular script feels vulnerable. Both my forms know language but we have been kept separate by lines drawn in ink.

Employment!

This word has been inscribed in blood on the forehead of our soul. This is the word that flows as blood in our veins. It is this word that appears as a dream to insult our sleep. Our souls feed on the fodder kept in the manger of a script yoked to this word—employment!

'The whole issue is not about Hindi-Urdu or about Hindu-Muslim, Balbhadra!' said Iffan. 'The issue is about employment. These days girls do not marry boys. Boys are only meant for affairs. Girls get married to jobs. Love is measured by a unit called salary and is now balanced on a scale called social position. You talk of Salima? Arre, no girl will ever marry you . . .'

Topi was very unhappy that night. He had finished writing Salima's thesis. He wished to pour his heart out to Salima. But what if Iffan was not saying the truth? What if she laughed at his outpourings?

Then on the day that Salima submitted her thesis, Topi told her, 'Come on, you treat me to a drink.'

'Right now I have to meet Mumtaaz aapa,' she said. 'There's a vacant room. Mitra Das has gone out on a holiday! For six months!'

Salima left.

The same thing happened several times. But Topi did not take it to heart. He did not tell Iffan about this out of fear that Iffan would laugh at him.

Then one day came the news that Wahid Anjum had left for Pakistan. He was heard making statements on Radio Pakistan and it became known that he had become a Vice-Chancellor.

And one day at the canteen, Salima said: 'Just think of that man's audacity. He wanted to marry me!'

'What is wrong in that?' asked Topi. 'Now he's become a Vice-Chancellor. Must be earning around two to three thousand.'

'Arre, what do you think—that I should get married to his job? Zakir Saheb has a job better than his.'

Topi felt quite excited on hearing this. Yet he had no courage to speak about his feelings for her.

'Why don't you take up a job or something somewhere?' asked Sakeena.

'I am t-trying,' stammered Topi. 'In some places I do not get a job because I am a Hindu and in some others because I am regarded as a Muslim.'

'But for how long can this go on?'

'I know,' said Topi. 'Can't go on like this forever.'

This happened on the day that Topi left for Benares to canvass for Kallan's elections.

On returning from Benares he learnt that Salima had married Wahid Anjum's job! He hadn't returned from Benares after some hundred or two hundred years. In just five days a story had taken a shortcut and reached its culmination.

At this juncture, the story-teller wishes to tell you something that even Topi does not know. It is that Iffan had not missed that train or anything of that sort. It was just that he did not wish to attend Salima's wedding at all.

'Idiot. Wanted to fall in love,' said Wajid. 'Why the hell are you standing here? Go get some tea,' Wajid screamed at the waiter. The Salima-Topi love affair and the Salima-Doctor Wahid Anjum wedding got drowned in the unfathomable well of the word 'idiot'.

This was what Topi liked best about Wajid. He knew how to bury the worst of moments with a casual heap of one expletive.

That's why after seeing Iffan off, Topi came to the canteen in the hope that his sorrows could be buried under one swear word from Wajid.

XVIII

W ajid Khan saw Topi and smiled . . .

His smile saddened Topi even further. He coughed, and pretending to
spit, turned his face away. In front of him was a lawn, basking in the filthy
moonlight.

Wiping his mouth and eyes with a kerchief, he entered the canteen. A
bulb saw its reflection on Jazabi's bald pate.

'Hello Bhai!' said Topi.

'Come,' said Wajid and turned his attention again towards Jazabi. 'So,
Jazabi Saheb, what I was saying was that the sweet sorrow that one finds
in Ghalib's poems—it is this sorrow that makes his poems so remarkable.'

'*Aadaab.*' Topi greeted Jazabi Saheb.

'So young man, how are you?' Displaying his unclean teeth, Jazabi
said, 'Has your Ifan Bhai left?'

'Not Ifan, Jazabi Saheb, it's Iffan,' said Topi. 'He is my friend. I can do
whatever I please with his name, not you.' He turned towards Wajid
Khan, 'Yaar, Wajid Bhai, continue with your monologue on Ghalib.'

Gradually, the evening's regular hangers-on arrived. There was a great
deal of talk about this and that but Topi's loneliness clung to him. In the
midst of the sea of all this talk and jokes and laughter, Topi stood quiet like
a solid rock of silence, allowing the noisy waves to beat all around him.

Then all of them left to see a Dara Singh film. Somehow or the other
minutes did pass by. But sooner or later Topi had to go back to that same
house—what else could he do? He went back to that house and wrapped
himself with a quilt. God knows why, but after all these years, Iffan's
Daadi came to his mind:

I don't tell you about what I've seen, I'm telling you about what I've heard. . . . Those who tell lies are damned. . . . Once upon a time there was an Emperor. He had seven daughters. One day as he was leaving on a journey, he called to his daughters and asked . . .

He could not sleep but exhaustion made him drowsy. Just before closing his eyes he decided that he would not live in Aligarh any longer. Then one morning, a postman who delivered express letters arrived. He rang the bell. It was a long time before Topi opened the door. He saw the envelope and closed the door.

After sometime, another postman came. He slipped an envelope through the aperture in the door.

Then came the sweeper. She kept ringing the bell but the door did not open. Then came the laundryman. He too went away after ringing the bell for some time.

By the time it was evening, the policemen arrived. The door was broken open. And then word went round that the man called Topi had become a corpse.

A sealed envelope was lying in the corridor. It bore a stamp from Jammu. The police opened that envelope but they could not understand its importance. There was a letter written by Sakeena and the letter had a raakhi wound round it.

The other letter too was found near Topi. That bore a post mark from Bahraaich. This one had been opened. It was a call for an interview. The police did not understand the significance of this letter as well.

The police carried out its routine enquiry. The corpse was dispatched for a post-mortem. The University was closed. A telegram was sent to Doctor Bhrugu Narayan of the Blue Oil. Ramdulaari too came along with him.

Along with Topi's belongings, Doctor Sahab also found Sakeena's envelope. He looked at the raakhi with disbelief. Ramdulaari started weeping all over again, lamenting all the time.

'Fa-hi-sha.' Doctor Saheb threw the raakhi as if it were a despicable object. There was certainly something in the tone of his voice that made Ramdulaari shut up and look at him.

'*Fahisha*'. Doctor Saheb said it again. Ramdulaari wished to say something in reply but she was not able to say anything, for she did not know what the word meant.

Topi too was one such word—a word whose meaning Ramdulaari did not know.

Glossary

Amaavat	solidified mango juice
Avataar	incarnation of God
Baaji	elder sister
Bahu	daughter-in-law
Baingan bharta	a dish made of brinjal
Baniya	generally merchant class
Barahsenis	an ethnic group; barah means twelve, shreni means orders/levels, seni means tray
Beta	son
Bhai	brother
Chaacha	uncle (father's brother)
Chapraasi	peon
Daada	paternal grandfather
Daadi	paternal grandmother
Dal	lentil
Do-ab	two rivers, the word Punjab is derived from Punj which means five and ab that means river. The Punjab is the land of five rivers.
Duvadas	twelve, duva is two and das means ten
Fahisha	disgraceful
Holi	festival of colours
Jeeja	sister's husband.
Kaalicharan	Kaali is the name of a goddess, charan means feet. So technically kaalicharan means someone who has surrendered himself at

	the feet of the goddess. But kaali also means black. Here it refers particularly to Topi's being dark complexioned.
Kaliyug	the fourth and last aeon of creation according to Hindu beliefs. This aeon is characterized by all that is against commonly-held core values. People belonging to this eon will be dishonest, unscrupulous, etc.
Kavi-sammelan	a gathering of poets where poems are read out.
Kirpaan	sword carried by Sikhs
Lakshmi	goddess of wealth
Lubz	means word in Urdu
Mamu	the word is Mama—means mother's brother, fondly referred to as Mamu.
Matti, makkhi, matthri, makkhan, maulvi	mud, flies, a savoury, butter and a Muslim scholar—the original words have been retained to maintain the alliterative nuance.
Miyaan	literally emissary, but used colloquially as mate or buddy, or some caste groups as standing for Muslim
Moong dal	green lentil
Mullah	Muslim priest
Mushaaira	an Urdu word for a gathering of poets where Urdu couplets are sung.
Nana	maternal grandfather
Namaaz	prayers said by Muslims
Pandit/Maulvi	Hindu and Muslim religious scholar/priest
Pooja	prayers offered by Hindus
Punj-ab	The land of five rivers
Raakhi	a silk thread that a sister ties on her brother's wrist as a token of her love and as an offering for their togetherness.
Raksha Bandhan	The festival day on which the Raakhi is tied. Raksha means protection and bandhan means bond. This is a festival that binds the sister and brother and where the brother accepts his responsibility to look after his sister.
Rasmulkhat	script
Roti	a kind of Indian bread made from wheat
Ser	unit of measurement
Shankar-Bhola	Both names refer to Lord Shiva, Bhola also means innocent.
Sherwani	a long shirt/kurta that falls down to the knees, now regarded largely as a traditional wear for Muslim men.

Sirfal	a fruit tree
Sohni	Punjabi folk legend (Sohni-Mahiwal), equivalent to Romeo Juliet
Takhallus	when the poet's name appears in his own poem
Tilva	sweetmeat made of sesame
Yaar	friend
Zamindar	landlord